To Bill Carrozza with Best wishes

DAGO RED! WESTWARD - HO!

By Bruno Buti

"Hail to the winemaker to whom we Plight our troth!!"

Salute!
Bruno Buti
12/12/04

A quote from the past:

"CHI NON PUO RIDERE A LA VITA,
NEANCHE SE LA MERITA"

Translation:

"HE WHO CANNOT LAUGH AT LIFE,
DOES NOT DESERVE ONE."

RAPE OF THE LAND

Born purebred Indians, natives of an ancient tribe,
A civilization that to Nature's laws did abide.

Our being, our purpose is decreed by our Gods,
To survive the elements against all odds.

From the land we take only that needed to sustain,
A lifestyle that causes no harm to the terrain.

We know that the abundance we have this day,
If not cared for now, will be lost along the way.

But now we have strangers invading our land,
They kill, plunder, leaving nothing but sand.

For the sake of profit-enrichment-outright greed,
Relentlessly raping, taking more than they need.

They make treaties and false promises galore,
But they are liars and cheaters, rotten to the core.

So now we'll have nothing and neither will they,
All because Nature's laws they refuse to obey.

Bruno

DAGO RED! WESTWARD -HO!

Copyright 2002, by Bruno O. Buti - Author
Registered ® Library of Congress
All rights reserved

Without limited rights under copyright reserved above,
no part of this publication may be reproduced, stored in
or introduced into a retrieval system, or transmitted
in any form or by any means
(electronic, mechanical, photocopying, recording, or otherwise)
without the prior written permission
of both the copyright owner and publisher of this book.

Jacket Design and Illustrations: Dug Waggoner
Word processing/Co-editor: Marisa Murphy

*For information regarding this publication, please
contact the publisher:*

Buti Publications, P.O. Box 304, Cloverdale, CA 95425
Tel. 707-894-5875, Fax 510-278-2438
e-mail: Prunesbb@aol.com

ISBN# 0-9648960-7-9

DEDICATION

In memory of the American Indian, their forefathers, their Holy Spirits, and their:

"Culture Lost"

In a state of wonder, I gaze upon the lands,
Where my forefathers, the Indians, once lived in bands.

Subsisting on buffalo, antelope, deer and birds,
As they migrated with the seasons in flocks and herds.

Following the sun over sand and rough terrain,
The rawness of this harsh land they did sustain.

Endeavoring to keep it in its natural state,
As did their forefathers for their children's sake.

Disturbing nothing, their presence hardly ever known,
For they loved these lands, it was their home.

They fought battles to protect what was rightly theirs,
But finally succumbed to the progress of invaders that didn't care.

Now that my people are gone and their culture lost,
It's finally realized that white man's progress came at a terrible cost.

The whispering winds say, the Spirits of my ancestors still dwell,
Above these once beautiful lands that now look like hell.

ACKNOWLEDGMENT

There is no question that the Indian tribes of this Nation, the United States of America, were devastated by the one-sided treaties and policies set forth by our government and the arrogance of those agencies that administered same. In truth, the American Indian was the least destructive to the environment and in no way ever squandered the natural resources of the lands they occupied, whereas just the opposite is true with the so-called industrious White Man.

The Indians took only what they needed for their subsistence, whereas the White Man took for profit, greed and enrichment, and in so doing not only devastated the resources of the land, but also displaced these true Americans, the Indians, causing them much needless suffering and the demise of their culture.

To these true Americans, the Indians of this Nation, who fought so hard way back then to preserve and protect these lands, the very thing we are now trying to do some 200 years later, to whom we owe an apology, with sincerity in our hearts: "We salute you."

To those Italians that chose to bring to these lands their skills and expertise in many fields, their contribution to the arts, music, culinary, viticulture and winemaking to name a few of their achievements, with hat in hand we say: "Thank you for coming."

And to the many pioneers of whatever ethnic background that blazed the trails and endured the hardships of their task, to tame and settle the Wild West, let their sacrifices be noted and not forgotten: "Amen."

PREFACE

The author, first generation born in America to Italian immigrant parents, applies his wildest, run-amuck imagination in telling this fictitious, idiotic tale in hopes of being entertaining and for no other reason. Therefore, hopefully, the reader, if in fact is of American Indian, Anglo Saxon or of Italian extraction, and as depicted in this story, whatever their religious faiths and spiritual beliefs may be their preferred system of worship, whether or not it be archaic, illusionary belief of receiving mandates manifested by some mystic source or Almighty God himself, but seen and heard only by some self-proclaimed Lord's Advocate with supposed prophetic powers, will not take offense to the manner in which these ethnic groups and their religious beliefs are portrayed.

In truth, it is doubtful that during those trying and difficult times (the early to mid-1800s) would these people (the characters of the story) conduct, talk or act as they are depicted. If anything, it would be assumed to be to the contrary. But then, diverse ethnic groups on a collision course, knowing nothing about each other's cultures, who is to say how they'd react when encountering each other out on the lonely, vast plains and prairies of the Western United States.

As for the risque, profanity-punctuated dialogue between the Indians as translated and applied in this story, it is assumed that they, in their own language and manner, did to some extent as did the White Man, express themselves accordingly. Since wild imagination has been applied by the writer, hopefully the reader will not take offense in the manner it is used. The names, characters, places, dates and incidents are used fictitiously, and resemblance to actual persons, living or dead, or to events or locales are coincidental.

INTRODUCTION
Moving Out West

In the early to mid-1800s, many pioneers made their way across the plains and prairies of this continent, North America, in caravans made up of covered wagons (prairie schooners), each carrying possessions and supplies according to their ethnic background and culture.

Much has been written about these people, their origin, lifestyle, religious beliefs, hardships and experiences along the way, and their encounters with the American Indian. However, in these writings, seldom if ever was there any mention of Italians. Maybe it was because there weren't any amongst these pioneers, or at least by what is known, no such caravans made up entirely of Italians. But suppose there was such a caravan? And as fate might have it, found themselves traveling west along with a wagon train made up entirely of Anglo Saxons who harbored unfavorable prejudices towards them, such as they did the Indians. And the American Indian, often referred to as the "Red Skin," who was forever at odds with the so-called "White Man," but now comes in contact with this new group of people, the Italians, often referred to as "Dagos," but finds them to be different and more to their liking, especially since they possessed, and shared, what they believed to be the nectar of life, wine "Vino" or as otherwise referred to amongst many wine drinkers as "Dago Red."

This story attempts to bring it all together as it might have been, but in a humorous way. Therefore, this fictional tale must not be construed as based on any factual event, but rather, be accredited to the vivid imagination of a writer of Italian extraction.

Dago Red! Westward - Ho!

CHAPTER 1

Loosening its grip on the frozen Missouri River, the crushing-crackling sound of thawing ice announced the end to a bitter winter. The Pioneers standing on the river's west bank bore witness to this spectacular phenomenon; winter in its last throes of death, giving way to the glorious birth of spring. As awesome as it appeared, nevertheless a welcomed sight. They'd been camped on the west side waiting anxiously for the coming of spring so they could embark on the long journey that lie ahead, moving out West. For most, it would be the last they'd ever see of St. Joseph, the bustling city on the east side of the river, a civilization where law and order prevailed and ended, the gateway to the wild and unruly West.

Here on the west side in a spectacular display of activity, the gathering of freight wagons and covered wagons of various descriptions (otherwise known as prairie schooners), drawn by horses, mules and oxen, along with their handlers busying themselves with last-minute details, inundated the landscape. Lured by the wild stories of riches and abundant land, they came from all parts of the country and were of many different ethnic backgrounds and cultures, but all with a purpose, a new life and enrichment, any way they could get it.

However, they were not about to set out on this treacherous journey in a helter-skelter manner. The purpose of this gathering was to form a caravan. As a large single unit, they'd stand a better chance against the perils of the journey. The responsibility of organizing and controlling the caravan fell upon the shoulders of a man under contract with the United States government as a guide, his main purpose, and being paid accordingly. But as it is when there is no previously appointed leader, and in this case being a habit with this particular person of taking the position to do so, declaring himself of government issue, therefore appoints himself as Wagon Master, the Commander, no less. No one had given much thought to the idea until he'd come along, but there he was, and he was the best qualified to lead the caravan across the treacherous trail leading west. They knew the going would be tough. There were treacherous rivers with raging currents and pockets of quicksand to cross, snake-infested swamps, wild animals, poison water holes, to name a few of nature's elements they'd have to deal with along the way. There were also the perils of man himself to contend with; highway robbers, murderers, hostile Indians determined to quell this overwhelming tide of intruders taking over their lands, and religious fanatics who chose to interpret religious writings in a fashion to fit their personal selfish egos and pleasures. Last but not least, disputes and squabbles within the ranks of the caravan itself.

Although they knew very little about the man other than his having done this before and, therefore, fully aware of the perils and how to deal with them, no one challenged his claim to authority. Besides, his bullying, nasty disposition and obnoxious manner was something no one cared to deal with or challenge. So without the benefit of a vote of confidence, the self-appointed Wagon Master, the man called Harvey, took full command and immediately got with it. With a heavy western-accented, stern, drawling vocabulary, he called for a gathering of the elders and proceeded to give the order of the day:

"All ya uns so-called elders best listen carefully as to wot ah got ta say. Ya git yur folks rounded up an ready to move out come mornin'. We uns ain't got no time to waste. Git them wagons all lined up one behind tuther. Ah wants the hoss drawn schooners in the lead, follered by thems dang ornery mules. Do ah make maself clear?" The statement was punctuated by his pulling back the flap of his duster, thus exposing his holstered gun and blood-encrusted knife.

The elders were stunned. For a moment they stood in silence. The order had come across in a no nonsense military fashion, something they hadn't anticipated. They expected to be asked rather than ordered. They wondered:

"Did this man's constant exposure to the harshness of the Wild West turn him into some sort of fanatical maniac?" A more chilling thought crossed their minds; the pelts tied to his saddle: "Were they Indian scalps?" The answer was obvious; in addition to all else, this man was a fierce Indian fighter as well, a man to be reckoned with. The answer to his question was a solemn:

"Yes, we understand."

The Wagon Master continued:

"Which one of ya' is in charge of thet mess o' oxen over yonder?" Along with the statement, he pointed to a group situated across the meadow away from the others.

The elders looked at each other, and to the last man shrugged their shoulders with an added response:

"It ain't none of us."

"Dang it!" cursed the Wagon Master. "Ah said ah wanted ev'ry one here!"

"Well, maybe they don't intend to be a part of the caravan," offered one of the elders.

Irritated with the thought, the Wagon Master barked in response:

"They's nobody in this meadow that's not in ma' caravan!

They's all in ma' jurisdiction. As much as ah hate them's dang foot-draggin' oxen, they's in the caravan, ah'll see to that!"

"They will slow us down, Mister Harvey. I think . . ."

"Ah'll do the thinkin!" cut in the Wagon Master, then added, "They'll take up the rear. Go tell em!"

"Sir, it may be best that you tell them since you have the authority."

"Ya dang well raht ah have, and ah'll do just that if'n they ain't gettin' with it, pronto!"

The positioning of the wagons as ordered was deemed to be proper. To this the elders did agree. In order not to impede the progress of the wagon train once underway, the horse-drawn schooners and wagons being escorted by men on horseback in the lead, followed by the Missouri contingency with their mules following made sense. The mules being smarter than the horses, if placed in the lead they might balk when encountering hazardous obstacles, whereas they would not if following the horses. And so by evening, after much ado and frustration, positioning of the wagons was done. That is, with the exception of the group camped off to one side, well away from the others, whose elder was not present when the order was given.

This particular encampment made up of some dozen schooners and several fully-loaded, heavy-duty freight wagons, showed no sign of activity that would indicate any intent to positioning themselves in line along with the others. Unlike their charged-up counterparts across the meadow, these people in the glow of campfires could be seen going about their affairs while laughing, singing and dancing to the beat of concertinas, guitars and mandolins, while their beasts of burden, pure white oxen, and domestic animals grazed contentedly nearby.

These people were Italians, and this was their custom, to live tranquilly, to live life to its fullest, no matter what the circumstances or wherever they may be. They had immigrated from Italy to work in big cities like New York, practicing their trades as stone mason, brick layers, tile setters and the like, but at cheap wages and in bad working and housing conditions. Needless to say, established Anglo Saxon construction contractors exploited them mercilessly. Those that survived the hazards of their jobs or falling from high rickety, makeshift scaffolds, the pelting of bricks and spilled mortar (at times wheelbarrow included), cascading down upon them from above, thus sweeping them off their perch and down into fresh batches of suffocating concrete, understandably chose to head west. Regardless of its hazards, it could hardly be much worse than what they were exposed to working at their trade in the big cities. Partly by nature and partly because of the joy of being freed from the clutches of unscrupulous work contractors, they reveled in festive delight, giving no thought to the others or to who was in command, if in fact, there was such a person.

From across the meadow, the Wagon Master, while putting the finishing touches to the chore of getting his own stuff organized and ready to strap onto his pack horse, the extent of his outfit aside from his saddle horse, by the light of the campfire's glow glanced in the direction of the festive group and in doing so, uttered profane, derogatory remarks about their conduct. Their indifference towards him trampled upon his ego. He could opt to pull out without them, but then, since the government paid him according to the wagon count at time of departure, it would cost him money if they were not a part of the caravan. However, once underway, no matter who or how many dropped out of the caravan, he'd be paid anyway. So, regardless of his frustration and the built-up animosity towards these people, he was determined to get them joined up in his caravan whether they liked it or not. To bolster his authority, he strapped on his bullet glistening gun belt and sheathed knife. Then in a growling, menacing manner, announced his intentions to the pioneers standing around within earshot:

"Dang em! Ah'm a gonna break up that party'n raht here 'n now. They's won't a-be dancin' when ah gits thru with 'em, by Gawd!" Following the statement, he popped the cork out of a whiskey bottle he was holding.

The elders watched in astonishment as he took a long, gulping draw from the whiskey bottle before tucking it back into his saddlebag. Not bothering to wipe the slobbered whiskey off his beard, he then brazenly marched off stiff legged across the meadow while loosening the hold-down strap of his holstered gun.

"My God!" exclaimed an elder, "Did you see that? What's this man have in mind? This is bad, we better stop him!"

"No!" responded another, "I've seen this sort of thing before. You interfere now and in his state of mind, whiskeyed up as he is, the embarrassment of having to back down will cause him to do the very thing you don't want him to do. Just hope those people over there, whoever they are, use their heads."

Huddled together at the edge of the campfire's glow, the pioneer elders, daring not to intervene, watched and waited for the outcome of an anticipated confrontation about to take place.

Music drifting across the meadow punctuated with singing and laughter in a language unfamiliar to the Wagon Master added to his contemptuous disposition. With every step of his heavy booted, swaggering gait, his duster flopped open exposing his holstered hogleg (six shooter) and scabbard, blood-encrusted knife, giving testamentary proof of its use as a tool for scalping Indians.

Framed against the glow of campfires beyond, the Wagon Master loomed up out of the darkness and stepped into the glow of the Italians' campfires. The music and dancing, as did the frolicking of youngsters, stopped abruptly.

They'd never seen such a person before. His duster exaggerating his already massive frame, sweat-saturated ten-gallon hat sitting atop a mop of unkempt hair adding the better part of a foot to his height, rumpled trousers tucked into size 13 leather buckled, mud splattered boots, and bearded as he was, struck the fear of death amongst them. He sensed their fear, he'd taken them by surprise.

A quick scan through penetrating, observing eyes revealed the absence of guns and so he cracked a death-defying smile; this was to his liking; they were at his mercy. For a moment he stood with spread legs viewing his short-statured adversaries in neat trim clothing, alpine hats cocked to one side and adorned with colorful chicken feathers. Not much of a match for him were they to flaunt his self-proclaimed authority or his vices, rape being one of them a sure giveaway by the gleam in his devilish eyes as he scanned the bosomy, sparkling dark-eyed, pitch-black haired, colorfully dressed women, the many children underfoot attesting to their sexual traits. This scoundrel hadn't missed a thing, and neither would he hesitate to impose his many vices upon them, given the opportunity. However for the moment, he'd concentrate his greedy thoughts on getting these people to shape up and join the caravan.

In a tone of pride, and loud enough to be heard clear across the meadow, he announced:

"Ah'm Mister Harvey! And ah'm in command! Ya all unnerstan?"

"Si . . . Si, you are El Commandante," responded the group meekly and in unison.

"Thet's fahn, jest fahn," said the Wagon Master.

Stepping forward, the one man who was best qualified to represent the Italians, not only because he was the oldest among them, but also because of his leadership qualities and because he spoke and understood English better than the others, "Giuseppe," also referred to as "El Capo," in his traditional, respective manner addressed the much taller and bigger than himself, Mister Harvey:

"Sir Commandante, how can we serve you?" he asked with eyes affixed to the every twitch and expression of the whiskey-reeking Wagon Master. He was alert, taking no chances. There was something in the tone of this man's voice that didn't quite set too well with him. Observing the Wagon Master's every move, he waited.

Chomping down hard on a slab of chewing tobacco, while munching it, in a bellow akin to a distraught cow searching for her wayward calf, Mister Harvey, the self-designated Commander, blurted:

"Ah have the auth-or-ity and ah'm in charge here an ah ain't about to tol-er-ate dis-o-be-dience. So, ah'm a gonna tell ya oncet an only oncet. Ya git thems thar wagons of ya-un over yonder tuther side of this dang meadow and take up the rear of'n the car-van. Ya'll is a gonna foller those dang ornery mules. Now dang it, git with it! Ya hear!" he said right to the point.

The Italians, whose way of life and culture included the consumption of wine and, to a degree, cognac, therefore making them somewhat authoritative in the matter of alcohol consumption, concluded that this man barking at them had been drinking and was somewhat short of being sober, in itself a matter to be reckoned with. Assuming the man to be speaking in English, or at least a variation thereof, if in fact the garbled burst of drawled profane-punctuated statement that sounded more like the growling bark of a rabid dog could be called either, the Italians applying their talent of communication with facial expressions coupled with hand gestures and mispronounced words, let it be known that aside from his being in command, they hadn't understood much of what was expected of them.

Followed by a gob of tobacco-laced spit the likes of which, if not the volume of it, certainly the putridness of it, could easily flatten a colony of prairie dogs from ten paces, the Wagon Master, towering a good two feet taller than his adversaries, now realizing that they were not as well versed in English as he was, in frustration blasted them again. Only this time, with added gestures. Left arm stretched out over the heads of his audience, index finger pointing in the direction of their wagons, right arm stretched out in the opposite direction across the meadow in the direction of the mule skinners, once again he barked:

"Now ya danged for-in-ers better git this straight, cuz ah ain't a gonna tell ya agin! Ya hear'n me? Git thems thar wagons therun an take em over yonder to where ah'm a point'n, behind thems danged on-ery mules and pull em up good'n tight!"

Other than the waving hand gestures, the only portion of the statement that came close to understanding was "good and tight," of which they misinterpreted as: "goodnight." They, therefore, responded accordingly with broad smiles, and waved back while repeating over and over again the word: "goodnight." Although not to his liking, they'd given it their best shot.

Enraged beyond comprehension, the Wagon Master while mumbling obscenities stomped out of the encampment and in measured strides, strutted back across the churned up, ankle deep mud which was once a grassy meadow, heading straight for the pioneers gathered around their campfires wondering and waiting. While the Wagon Master made his way across the meadow, the Italians gathered around their arm waving, oratorizing Capo Giuseppe in hopes of getting a better grasp of what was expected of them. However, it was to no avail for he was just as dumbfounded as they. But his teenage daughter, Giuseppina, seventeen years old and at the threshold of womanhood, who had schooling in this new land, America, and who was listening in attentively, could possibly translate, or at least decipher the western, if not barbaric, Wagon Master's vocabulary. In his native tongue, her aging father asked:

"Giuseppina my child, what did the man say? What does he want us to do?"

All fell silent. The arm waving stopped. They eagerly waited for the answers to the girl's father's questions. But in the textbooks she'd studied, nowhere was there anything relating to the English language such as was spoken by the Wagon Master. She was as much in the dark as the rest of them. In her native tongue, while shrugging her shoulders, she answered the first question:

"Papa, I don't know what he said. I couldn't understand him," she stated with puzzled expression.

"What do you mean, you can't understand! It is English, is it not?" he demanded to know.

"But Papa, I don't think it's English," she pleaded. "He speaks a strange language."

"Well, what do you know about that? We came all the way out here and what do we get? A foreigner in charge that can't speak the language."

The escalating chatter and arm waving that followed was put to rest with a stern command:

"Everybody, shut up! We must think, not talk!"

After his people finally quieted down, the old man again addressed his daughter:

"Giuseppina," asked her father, "surely there was something in what he said that would indicate what he wants from us...no?"

"Well, he did mention mules, and he was pointing to our wagons and those over there, and they are all getting together and lining up, so maybe he wants us to move over there with them?"

An exulting response rose up from the gathered crowd. Yes, that was it, she'd guessed it right. Her father was pleased but added a cautious, sobering warning:

"That man likes whiskey and carries a gun. We must be careful not to antagonize him. I don't think he likes us."

They again fell silent as they faced reality; it was not the harshness or challenges of the Wild West, but rather, the animosities towards them as Italians that concerned them.

"Dang them thar for-in-ers!" cussed the Wagon Master as he approached the pioneers. "Wot in hell are theys doing out here if'n theys cain't speak a decent inglish. This'n ain't no dang carnival tur we's a'goin on!" he blurted in contempt of his charges he'd just chastised.

"Do you think they'll be giving you much trouble?" asked Elder Jake, the mule skinner.

"Givin me trouble?" snapped back the Wagon Master in a wide-eyed expression of surprise.

"Theys ain't a gonna give me no trouble, ahs the one thets gonna give them trouble. Ah cain't stan thems for-in-ers any mor'n ah can stand thems stinkin' Red Skins. Ah cain't wait til thems dang injuns catches up to 'em. Theys'll lern 'em a thing or two, by Gawd!" As he made the statement, he gave a nod and shift of eyes towards his saddle to call attention to the many Indian scalps tethered to its strappings. To the pioneers, the point was made. They shuddered at the thought of a confrontation with Indians.

To the relief of the pioneers, activity across the meadow indicated that the Italians were in fact preparing to move their outfit over to their side, join the main body of the caravan in accordance with the Wagon Master's wishes, but he showed no emotion or satisfaction but rather grumbled in disgust:

"Lookie that, more dang stuff'n such that theys'll ever need. Thems oxens is a gonna kill themselves a pull'n thems heavy wagons acrost country."

Jake the mule skinner concurred with the added comment:

"What's with that huge bronze bell they're hauling a-sett'n there on that sturdy wagon? Darn thing must weigh a ton. They'll play hell getting that thing across country, Indians or no Indians, don't you think so. . . Mr. Harvey?"

"That's for dang sure! But ah'll be danged if'n ah'm a gon' back thar an try to convince them's tutherwise! Ah talked to 'em in plain inglish and theys didn't unnerstand a dang word ah say'd! They'd ought to know better than try to haul thet thar kind of weight acrost country! Anyways, theys all be tak'n up the rear, an ya needn't wait on 'em! If'n they's cain't keep up, ta hell with 'em!" slobbered the Wagon Master.

The bell was not only heavy but also quite unusual in its configuration. Its girth, some 20 inches in diameter, was quite narrow in relation to its 5 foot length with the sound bow flaring out a mere 26 inches in diameter at the lip. Resting horizontally cradled on wooden beams with its mouth facing to the rear extending past the wagon's tailgate gave it the appearance more of a cannon cast in the foundries of Scotland than a bell. Heavy duty block and tackles with their accompanying ropes of extreme length hanging on the sides of this artistically hand-painted, sturdy wagon gave credence to the weight of its cargo. Since the extra space around the bell was utilized to store and transport bocce balls (appearing as cannon balls) and containers of polenta and pasta neatly stacked behind the bell (appearing as canisters of gun powder), the whole configuration did, in fact, take on the appearance of a war machine.

Another wagon of similar description parked alongside

Dago Red! Westward - Ho!

the bell wagon hadn't gone unnoticed either. Only this one was loaded with unusually large oak barrels exceeding the normal 50 gallons, full to capacity. The Wagon Master had something to say about that also:

"Damned fools, carry'n all that water fer naught! Lookee that load of barrels, and if'n that ain't enough, lookee whats hangín on them thar schooners! They'll be laggin' behind, carry'n all that thar weight! They'd best not be givin' me no bad time on the trail, by Gawd!" he growled as he spat.

One of the mule skinners who was standing around sizing up the situation of the barrel wagon as well as the extra barrels strapped to the side of the schooners, with a cocked eye, while nodding his head in the direction of the barrel wagon, then again towards the schooners, posed a question directed to the elder of the horse drawn schooners as he walked up, wondering about the little people as well. Since he was known to be an ordained Presbyterian Elder, he was addressed accordingly.

"Elder Jeb," he said, "do you suppose we should take heed to all that water they're carrying? Maybe they know something we don't know?"

The question had merit since by what it appeared, the oxen group was indeed carrying much more water than what was normally needed. In a thoughtful manner while scratching his chin, Elder Jeb answered:

"Ya know, considering the way they're acting, the music, their dress, hardly speaking English, the bell and all, I believe they're Italians, Catholics at that. Yup, I'm sure of it, that's what they are all right. As for all that water, well, I can't explain that. But I can tell ya this: them Indians are gonna have a ball with those little people, what with no guns to speak of, slow moving oxen, bogged down with all that weight. I kinda feel sorry for them little fellers," sighed the elder while shaking his head in disbelief.

"So that's what they is," put in the Wagon Master. "Ah'd hear'd of 'em but never did seed 'em. Whaddaya know, I-talians, Dagos, Cath-o-lics at that. Dang fools, couldn't tell 'em a thing. They's no idea what it's all about . . . too bad," he said somewhat gleefully.

The mention of Catholics brought on a comment from a Methodist traveling alone, a self proclaimed man of the cloth himself, called: "Reverend Gadwall," a plump sort of fellow, as big around as he was tall that left the impression that he'd never missed a meal and that he sat more than he stood:

"Hmmm...Catholics you say?" he said in a manner as if to raise a question. "Oh well, they are Christians, in a way, that is. Maybe God will intervene . . . providing . . .?" His short sermon finished, he bid the others, "goodnight."

The Wagon Master, letting fly a gob of repulsive chaw, wiping the tobacco juice from his beard onto the sleeve of his leather duster, addressed Elder Jeb:

"Jeb," he drawled, "ya best git that pee-ano of you'rn strapped down good'n proper. Thars some purty ruff go'ins out thar."

That, of course, was good advice since the heavy piano was resting up against the tailgate of the wagon. A sudden jar could cause it to bust off the tailgate completely and topple off the wagon.

"I'll do that," responded Elder Jeb, then followed with a sincere word of advice of his own: "You know, Mister Harvey, I suggest you smile when referring to them Italian people over there as "Dagos" while in their presence. I've heard they can get quite rough when insulted."

Ignoring the comment, giving one last glance to see that all was in readiness, and being it was late evening, the Wagon Master addressed the few remaining elders that had gathered:

"A-gettin' late, best we'uns turn in. We'uns'll be on the trail come first light." With that, they all went their separate ways.

Dago Red! Westward - Ho!

Little did they know the Italian's reason for their unorthodox actions, or better put, their way of life. In no way would they consider settling down as a community without the means of communicating with God, the ringing of the bell to announce the saying of Mass. After transporting it all the way from Italy, they were not about to leave it behind now, come hell or high water.

And the wagon load of barrels, oak barrels of European manufacture, 230 liter capacity, were full of wine, not water as believed by this ill-tempered heathen, the Wagon Master that unless he soon changed his ways, he'd surely be condemned to hell! Wine, the symbol of blood amongst Christians, needed for sacramental purposes to cleanse the soul, thus preparing it for its long but joyous journey to the Promised Land, Heaven. Its nutritional value, its adhesive properties that bring together and hold people of all ethnic backgrounds in good fellowship, its contribution to inspiring love and affection of the opposite sex, man and woman, that bring forth children, the fruits of love. Oh yes, if this be known, these western roughnecks would surely take heed of the Italian's way of life.

As for the extra barrels strapped to the covered wagons, in this case they'd guessed right; it was water, more than enough if it were not for the fact that the extra water was needed to preserve the bundles of Zinfandel grapevine cuttings, wrapped in burlap, packed in damp sawdust, constantly dabbed with water not only to keep them from drying out, but also to effect cooling through the evaporation of the water, a natural refrigeration process known and handed down for many centuries by these so-called misguided people, the Italians.

CHAPTER 2

Come first light next morning, the caravan made up of horses, mules, oxen and with the exception of the Italians who for the most part walked along with their animals, men mounted on horseback along with the Wagon Master in the lead, stretched out single file for the better part of a mile as they headed due West. On occasion the Wagon Master in all his glory, gun belt glistening with bullets and its leather holster cradling a six-shooter slung low so its handle could be palmed instantly when need be, scalps tied to his saddle strappings to impress his charges, galloped along the line urging the stragglers to tighten it up, something the Italians with their slow moving oxen could not do. As if intentionally, he made it a point to push the main caravan hard, thus creating an even bigger gap between them and the Italians. It was obvious, his intent was to out-pace them. To him, they were inferior people, and therefore wished them to be as far behind the main group as possible, lose them altogether if he could.

By midday on the next day, the main caravan at the constant urging of the Wagon Master to push their teams to the limit, was miles ahead of the Italians. In contrast to their counterparts, the Italians trudged along casually with their slow but steady moving oxen. The barrel wagon as was the wagon bearing the bell taking up the very rear, were each hitched to no less than a team of eight of these massive, white beasts of burden. At all times, their handlers bearing 6 foot walking staffs made of solid hickory, walked alongside the oxen constantly giving verbal instructions rather than using reins and whips such as the pioneers, thus keeping up a steady pace without fatigue or anxiety. Come sundown, the main body, as did the Italians still lagging well behind, settled down for the night.

Next morning at the crack of dawn both groups were back on the trail. Again the Wagon Master pushed the main body hard, and gave no heed to the comments and concerns of the pioneer elders:

"We're pushing too hard, running our animals into the ground." Nor did he give a damn that the Italians were falling further and further behind; if anything, he gloated. When concerns were expressed, he put them down with stern reprimands:

"Ah'l worry bout the dang Dagos. Ya keep up the pace, keep movin'!" he shouted while riding back and forth along the line.

"Mr. Harvey, look at the horses, all sweated up like that ... we're killing 'em! And them mules back there are just as bad. We have to slow it up a bit!" pleaded Elder Jeb.

"Ah say'd keep it up, dang it! Ah mean wot ah say'd!"

There was no question, Harvey was the commander, and command he did.

After Harvey galloped off, Elder Jeb's son John, a strapping young man 18 years of age, reined his horse up alongside his father:

"Dad," he said, "do we have to put up with that . . . that kind of talk?"

"I know what you're thinking, son, but at least for the time being, let it be."

Come evening the pioneers made camp, as did the Italians now several miles apart. While the womenfolk prepared the evening meal, the men worked feverishly rubbing down their stressed draft horses. In their sweaty condition the chilling night air would stiffen them up, a serious matter for sure. In contrast, the Italians were not faced with the same problem. Their oxen were not sweated up. They grazed leisurely, contentedly, soothed by the soft strumming of guitars and the gently plucked strings of the mandolins. Music rippled through the hearts of the womenfolks, thus arousing the loving warmth within them. An added goblet of wine was all that was needed to assure an exciting but relaxing evening.

Next morning, by the time the sun's rays splashed across the prairie's sea of wild oats, the Italians in their casual mode of travel, were well on their way, but not so with their counterparts up ahead. Their teams were beat, fatigued and, for that matter, so were their handlers. They'd worked half way through the night grooming, walking their draft animals, horses and mules alike least they'd cool too fast and get stiff and cramped up. The elders faced up to the Wagon Master:

"They'd have to sit out the day or risk losing the animals." Reluctantly he agreed, and so while the pioneers went about their chores, the Wagon Master caught up on his drinking.

By mid-afternoon along came the Italians, strolling along, chatting, humming and singing, talking to their draft animals as they tramped along at a steady pace as though they were in an Easter Parade, following the well established trail of previous caravans moving West. The wine barrel wagon rumbling along sporting the Italian flag waving from the top of a staff secured to its side, followed by the bell wagon with the American flag in a similar fashion taking up the rear, creaking and groaning with every synchronized step of the team of massive oxen. Not bothering to stop, they cruised on by and passed the main group's encampment, waving and tipping their feathered Alpine hats, nodding their heads in a gesture of salutations to their counterparts, the pioneers who in turn responded in similar fashion, but in wonder.

Dago Red! Westward - Ho!

The rumbling and creaking coupled with the chatter awoke the Wagon Master from his alcohol-induced afternoon nap just in time to see the tail end of the bell wagon disappear from sight. Coming out of his stupor, staggering to his feet, he gazed in disbelief, spit out his chaw, then ran the full length of his arm across his tobacco-saturated mustache before bringing his vocal chords into play. In a garbled growl he cursed:

"How'n hell? Damned thems little Dago buggers!"

Readjusting his rotten smelling, sweaty ten gallon hat he added:

"Wot'n hells thems for-in-ers think thar do'n? Nobody moves out ahead unless ah'm ah tel'n em! Damned thems for-un Dagos!" he swore.

"Ah'l learn 'em!"

In a fit of rage, he grabbed his saddle by the horn and tossed it onto his horse minus the blanket. From force of habit, the Wagon Master then grabbed the saddle bags without giving thought of what might be in them, aggressively tossed them across the back of the saddle. Not until the half-empty bottle of whiskey that he had stashed into the bags just before he'd konked out earlier in the afternoon, did he realize his mistake. The jarring action ejected the bottle from the bag, sending it cartwheeling through the air, and smashing itself to pieces against a pile of boulders thus splattering whiskey helter skelter.

In an act of violence, he took out his misfortune on the horse by slapping the bags across his rump before tossing them aside. The horse shuddered as his master grabbed the dangling latigo strap, then pulling it up through the ring. As the cinch came in contact with his belly, the horse, knowing what his master in his present state of mind would do, took a deep breath to expand his belly to compensate for the strangling effect of the cinch as its latigo strap tightened with excessive force. The horse held his breath as his master jammed his boot into the stirrup, swung his right leg over and before his ass even hit the saddle, spurs dug into the horse's flank simultaneously with the lambasting, screaming order to move out fast.

"Giddy up, ya damned son-of-a-cayuse!" he yelled in flushed anger. The order was carried out to the letter. Exhaling the air from his lungs with a blasting snort, thus causing the cinch to go slack, now loose, poised hooves catapulted him into a frenzied gallop. With wide-eyes and flared nostrils, he charged through the camp scattering the panicked pioneers, sending them running for their lives least the crazed steed with a drunken heathen at the reins trample them to death.

Flailing the ground with pounding hooves, the galloping horse reached the trail within seconds, at which point he'd need to swing onto the trail heading West. With the loosening saddle bouncing his passenger even higher, crushing his testicles with every galloping surge, thus bringing about a screaming new command:

"Whoa! Damn it! Whoa!" but the steed paid no heed and leaned into the turn at full bore. Upon doing so, centrifugal force kicked into play, spinning the saddle around to the underside of the horse, thus catapulting the screaming rider headlong into full flight. Arms and legs spread out, duster flapping in the breeze, he sailed through the air like a flying squirrel leaping from tree to tree until he finally hit the ground head first. The sudden lightening of the load told the horse that something was wrong. Pulling up short, panting hard, he turned and trotted back to the scene of the disaster. Seeing his master rolling around writhing and groaning with pain sent shudders throughout his body. The horse knew he'd done wrong, but wasn't about to stick around for the reprimand that was sure to follow. Saddle dangling at his underside, wide eyed and frothing, he hightailed it back from whence he came, to the safety and sanctuary of the masses.

Having witnessed the sporting but disastrous event, the elders took off at a dead run to the aid of the Wagon Master, commenting as they ran side by side:

"We'll never make it to California at this rate," commented Elder Jeb. "That man, amongst other things, is just plain loco. We'd better talk some sense into him."

"Are ya pretty good with a six shooter?" asked Jake, the mule skinner.

"What in hell do you mean by that?"

"He ain't about to change his ways. Ya'll have to kill him, if'n he ain't already dead."

In addition to the elders, there were others rushing to the scene. Overtaking the lot of them was Reverend Gadwall. Shaped as he was, he appeared to be rolling rather than running, but regardless, to save the soul of this heathen it was imperative that he be there at the instant the stricken man cashed in his chips. For if he wasn't, Satan would surely beat him to it and impale his soul on the flaming tines of his pitchfork, toss him onto his wagon of despair and haul it down into Hell. Upon reaching the scene, panting like a wolf bitch in heat, Reverend Gadwall immediately took charge for there appeared to be no life left in the man that lay still at their feet:

"Step back! Everybody step back!" he ordered as he excitedly flipped through the weathered pages of the Bible he was carrying.

As ordered, everybody stepped back, took off their hats and waited in silence for the Reverend to administer the last rites, thus delivering Mister Harvey's heathen soul from the clutches of the Devil and into the hands of the Lord wherein, with enough scrubbing and scouring, it would be cleansed of the scum of his heinous past. But, by the time Reverend Gadwall found the page containing the passages necessary to perform the soul saving act, Mister Harvey stirred, rolled over and, in a glazed stare, peered at the crowd looking down at him. Indeed, he was not dead as first thought. In disgust, with bowed head and sunken feeling within, Reverend Gadwall slapped the Bible shut and substituted the last rites with a word of wisdom:

"Mister Harvey," he said, "I suggest you put more faith in the Lo..." Interrupted, the statement was concluded by an added word of wisdom from Jake, the mule skinner:

"Better, a mule."

Disgusted, Reverend Gadwall walked away mumbling:

"Of all the luck. A chance of a lifetime, to save the soul of a true heathen, has just slipped through my fingers!"

However, Reverend Gadwall wasn't the only one present to "fold up his tent," so-to-speak, and walk away disappointed. Satan, lurking nearby, was equally if not more so disappointed with the outcome for Mister Harvey was the perfect candidate to serve his purpose down in his Kingdom of Hell. He'd been scouring the countryside looking for just such a heathen with the expertise of Mister Harvey. He needed him to ride herd on the many top corporate executives, their colleagues and political buddies now residing in Hell that had screwed just about everyone on the face of the Earth and were now down in Hell wheeling and dealing, screwing the hapless, miserable, sweating commoners (sinners, such as themselves), the grunts that stoked the furnaces of Hell, out of their just due.

They were completely out of hand. Like greedy hogs with their feet in the trough, enriching themselves off the sweat of others. It was so bad that Satan, with all his expertise and power, could not stop them. He desperately needed a heathen the likes of Mister Harvey to rein them in lest they take over the whole of his Kingdom. Therefore he, too, having missed the opportunity of a lifetime, and the need to stick around no longer of eminent priority, Satan, the

Dago Red! Westward - Ho!

Devil, horns glittering vividly from the rays of the fires of Hell below, like the distinguishing flame of "Will-o-the-Wisp," receded back down into the bowels of the Earth.

By evening the next day, again being pushed to the brink of disaster, horses and mules alike sweating, frothing at the mouth, caught up to the slow moving, nonchalant, so-called foreigners, the Italians, and as could be expected the Wagon Master refused to recognize them as any part of his charges. He was through with them, and if they knew what was good for them, they'd stay clear of him. But regardless of the animosities towards them, the Italians were being nice to their tormentor. They even went through the usual courteous ritual of salutations as they were passed on by, and all they got in return from the Wagon Master was a gob of chewing tobacco splattered at their feet. However the pioneers, admiring the spunk of their adversaries, their resourcefulness, returned the courteous gesture with at least a wave of hand accompanied with a nod of recognition. Amongst themselves they commented:

"You know," said Elder Jeb as he reined his saddle horse alongside a fellow pioneer, "I kinda admire those little people. I think they know what they're doing, don't you?"

"Yep, I agree,' came the response. "And I gotta tell ya, they're gettin' there just the same without killing themselves."

After a few minutes of thought, the conversation drifted back to the incident of the previous day.

"I'm afraid Harvey is going to be a liability in the long run, or at least useless dead weight. Half the time he's drunk and obnoxious, a trait that I'm afraid out here in the West won't be tolerated. For one thing, scalping Indians for bounty is no longer allowed. It's obvious he's still doing it, for two reasons: I figure it's for "profit-bartering" and to satisfy his ego, "superiority."

"You may be right. I never looked at it that way, that's bad."

"You better believe it's bad. And those people we just passed back there, I've heard of them Italians. Don't let their courteous, carefree style mislead you. They can be your God-Sent Savior, but if you cross 'em, look out! If Harvey doesn't get off their back, sooner or later he'll get his ass kicked, and I mean good and proper."

Jeb's son injected his own thoughts to the conversation:

"And I'll be there to help them!" He had all the reason in the world to dislike Harvey, but not the Italians, especially Giuseppina. In passing, her jet black wavy hair swirling in the breeze, framed against the background of the pure white oxen as she strolled alongside them, stamped the image of a Goddess on his mind.

CHAPTER 3

And so for the next several weeks the now two distinct groups leap-frogged their way across the great plains, past Fort Kearney following the Platte River, heading West. The main group still under command of the irate Wagon Master who was forever pushing his charges, was causing time-consuming equipment breakdowns and keeping both man and beast constantly stressed and agitated and, therefore, never being able to shake the Italians who were forever overtaking them. In every instance that they passed each other, the Wagon Master went into a rampage. But because of the elders at times now challenging his authority, and the fact that he'd run out of whiskey, he did back down somewhat which made for improved conditions. Another reason that they were getting along better is because the elders, as well as all others in the caravan, were keeping their distance from Wagon Master Harvey. He'd never bathed or changed his clothes since they'd left St. Joseph, Missouri, and so stunk to high heaven. It got so bad that if it were not for his movements, he appeared more dead than alive to the extent that turkey vultures were swooping in on him, checking him out, believing that if he wasn't already dead, he soon would be.

Maintaining their lead, the main group now reached the rain-swollen South Platte River at Julesburg, where they'd now have to ford the muddy river, an easy task under normal conditions, but somewhat hazardous considering the high water. The little ferry at the crossing point, a makeshift contraption at best, was not of much use since it was never intended to be used to accommodate even one wagon the size of a prairie schooner, let alone a whole caravan of them. Therefore, the ferry tender, a man called Jason, well known to the Wagon Master, despite his ranting and raving would not budge from his position. The ferry was not to be used to transport the caravan across the river, and so stated:

"Dang ya, Harvey, you're as ornery as a mule and smell twice as bad. I told ya, I ain't gonna do it, and that's that! Take your danged wagons and cross downstream where it's shallower!"

"What? And git sucked in ta thet quicksand? Ya know's dang well it's plum full of pot holes big nuff to swaller up a schooner! In this high water, thems wagons'd never make it! And don't ya dang me, dang ya!" cursed the Wagon Master.

The elders, along with several others of their group, mule skinners alike, converged on the scene but didn't talk, just listened. The Wagon Master had been pushing them to near breaking point; they and their animals were beat, and in any case, in no condition to tackle the crossing before resting their draft animals or, for that matter, themselves. Attentively, they listened to the ongoing dispute between the Wagon Master and Jason the ferry tender.

"Quicksand or otherwise!" snorted Jason, "I ain't about to lose my ferry over the likes of you . . . pard! And if you weren't so damned scared of getting wet, you'd of already been across! Besides, you stink! For that alone I'd charge you double! That is if I had a mind to take your wagons across, which I don't!"

That final statement was the final straw. As true as it was, the Wagon Master nevertheless took it as an insult and demonstrated accordingly:

"Why, ya mangy ol' coot, highway robber, ah'v a mind ta toss ya into the drink!"

As the statement was made, he lunged at the tender

who, having experienced such confrontations before, aptly stepped aside, held out his foot, tripping his opponent, thus sending him headlong, rolling down the embankment and into the river. To add insult to injury, he then said:

"Take a bath while you're down there, ya need it!"

Scrambling down the embankment, the elders reached out with a helping hand to drag the sputtering Wagon Master out of the cold, murky waters. Once on dry land they were quick to remind him that, as they'd stated once before, he'd best get control of himself or they'd go on without him, that is, after resting a day or two before taking their chances of crossing the river further downstream. But, the Wagon Master, as soaked as he was, now being not only cool of body but also somewhat cooler of mind, offered some advice of his own:

"Ya try it an' thems thar danged ornery mules'll scatter thems wagons of yor'n from here to Kingdom Come! Go ahead! Try it! An' sees whats ya end up with! An don't ya forgit thet quicksand neither! It'll swoller the lot of ya!" he warned.

Taking an about face and now somewhat calmer himself, Jason the tender took up the Wagon Master's cause:

"Harvey's right!" he stated. "Mules are like cats, they don't like water, excepting for drinking. They'll balk sure as hell the first sign of trouble!"

The elders wondered. While in conversation between themselves, the tender interrupted with a suggestion:

"Why don't you folks just set a spell?" he asked. "The river'll be down again in a day or two, you can cross then."

"No! Dang it! We're in a hurry! Cain't wait! We'll figger out somethin'!" argued the Wagon Master.

"Harvey! Damn it! It makes sense! We'll wait!" stated Elder Jeb in a firm, authoritative manner.

Rather than challenging Elder Jeb and risk losing command, at least for the moment, the Wagon Master backed down.

"All right, it's yer call, they's yer'n wagons."

Now that things had calmed down, the elders went back to their people and prepared to make camp. The Wagon Master, not happy but nevertheless calmed down, and no worse off whether he be dry or wet, approached the tender who he knew from previous trips to be dealing in whiskey and pelts; doing business with the local Indians and whom ever, apologetically asked:

"Jason . . . my friend, ya wouldn't happen ta have a bottle er two of whiskey ly'n around thet ya'd be a will'n ta part with, would ya now?" he asked while leaning heavily towards the tender so as not to be heard by the others.

"It so happens I have, but I'm not your friend, ya'll have to pay for them! And I have to tell ya, Harvey, I have it to trade with the Indians, for pelts, so it's spiked with red hot pepper and a few yellow jackets thrown in to add a little "zest," ya know. They like it that way, fetches an extra pelt or two."

"Fine, ah'll take it! Fire water! Glory be! By Gawd, jest wat ah needs. Why, the last time ah partook to thet thar stuff, the next day it danged near set afire to my long johns, charged outta the privy and set in the river for the better part of the morn'n. But ah gots to have it. Can't make the trip without it."

The Wagon Master was indeed desperate. He hadn't had a swallow of whiskey in weeks. He was thirsty and water wasn't much to his liking.

"All right, that will cost ya ten dollars or I'll take three of them Indian scalps in trade. Which will it be?"

"Three scalps! Dang ya, Jason! Yur noth'n mor'n a son of a dang pole cat! Ya knows danged well them's injun scalps is worth a hell of a lot mor'n thet!"

"Take it or leave it!"

The more they hassled, the more the Wagon Master

yearned for the whiskey, until finally he gave in.

"Here, take the dang scalps. Thar's more injuns out thar! Ah'll get me some more . . . ah s'pose!"

"Good! Set a spell and we'll drink to the occasion," offered the tender, while flashing a set of tobacco-stained teeth.

"Provid'n yur buy'n."

"All right, ya cheapskate, so we'll drink my whiskey!"

CHAPTER 4

Due to the hangup at the ferry, the Italians, although moving at a snail's pace compared to the main group, came into view. The elders, the first to see them coming and fully aware that no way could they ever expect to ferry their bell and barrel wagons across the river, and the fact that the Wagon Master was still well saturated with whiskey, therefore unpredictable, decided to intercept them, explain the situation, and above all, keep them away from the ferry and the Wagon Master altogether, head them off.

"Jeb," inquired Jake the mule skinner, "do you think we can get the message across? You remember the difficulty Harvey had back at St. Joseph. Apparently they don't understand English."

Having joined in more so from curiosity than for any other reason, Reverend Gadwall added his two bits worth:

"Yes, and you best not forget, they are Catholics . . . you know," he warned.

"Yeah, well, let's give it a try anyway," answered Jeb.

"What do we have to lose?" With Jeb's son John tagging along, the men rode out to meet the caravan.

Upon approaching the Italian caravan they were impressed with the condition of their equipment, no sign of wear and tear, and the oxen especially, they noticed that the huge, massive animals didn't have an ounce of sweat on them, no bits in their mouths to strangle their tongues and bring about frothing like on the horses and mules. These animals were calm, tranquil and, like their handlers walking alongside, showed little if any sign of fatigue.

Dago Red! Westward - Ho!

Seeing their approach, the Italian caravan halted. The Capo Giuseppe along with several other men, his daughter Giuseppina at his side, stepped forward to greet the visitors. Although knowing of each other, both sides were meeting on a personal basis for the first time. With raised hand in a gesture of friendliness, Jeb extended a greeting. In like fashion, the greeting was returned. Before any words could be exchanged between the two leaders, the Capo, in his native tongue, asked his daughter:

"Giuseppina, see if you can find out what language they speak. You remember the trouble we had with the Commandante."

No sooner had she responded in her native tongue, Jake, the mule skinner, posed a question:

"Jeb," he said, "what language is that?"

"You heard what I told you!" butted in Reverend Gadwall. "I'd watch my step if I were you," he again warned.

Before Jeb could respond to either, Giuseppina exclaimed:

"Oh, you speak English! You must excuse us for speaking in our native Italian," she said apologetically.

"We thought that maybe you spoke the same language as Mister Harvey, the Commander. We could not understand him," she explained politely.

"Well, I'll be damned!" exclaimed Jeb as he swung out of his saddle while handing the reins to his son. Grinning, he stepped forward with extended hand, which was met with the Capo's extended hand. The handshake was genuine and sincere, and out here in the West, it meant something.

Frozen in the saddle, dumbfounded, John took the reins without realizing he had them. His lightly whiskered face could not hide the astonishing look it expressed as he gazed down beholding Giuseppina's sweetness and beauty. Coming out of his trance, he said:

"My name is John."

She responded softly with a smile and a sparkle in her eye: "My name is Giuseppina."

Fortunately for John lest he'd topple off his horse, his father came to his rescue by saying:

"We apologize for Mister Harvey's conduct. It is not to our liking, and that's why we stopped you. He's drunk! It is best that you camp back here. Besides, the ferry can't take you across, and the water is a little too high to cross today," advised Jeb.

"Ah, I see," said old Capo Giuseppe . "Well, we are not in a hurry; we'll cross tomorrow." Then, adhering to their native custom, extended an invitation:

"Come join us, as the animals are being tended to, we'll talk and have a glass of wine," he offered, extending the same to the others as well.

All but Reverend Gadwall accepted the invitation by swinging out of their saddles. He was not about to join in on what he believed to be a repulsive idea, drinking wine for whatever reason. To the disappointment of his pony, a short-legged, chubby little critter, the reverend did not dismount but instead, with the saddle buried in the mass of his ass, reined his mount to a backbreaking fast trot, thus hauling his carcass back to the main caravan. The reverend's flabby hulk draped over the stubby-legged pony gave the impression that the whole of the thing was moving along on ball bearings.

Without being told to do so, as was their custom, the womenfolks immediately set out to accommodate their guests by setting out trays of goodies, including dried plums, raisins, dried figs and nuts. Along with the snacks sitting on a cottonwood stump, they proceeded to draw goblets of wine from a spigot stuck in the head of a barrel at the barrel wagon. Noting the procedure, Jeb asked a question of his host:

"Are all those barrels full of wine?"

Dago Red! Westward - Ho!

"Yes, of course."

Giving the matter further thought, Giuseppe added:

"Well, maybe not all. We drink some every day . . . you know?"

"So now we know," thought Jeb as he scratched his chin in wonder. "Of course, Italians, wine, makes sense. And munching dried plums, fruit and nuts with an occasional sip of wine as they walk along, constantly nourishing their bodies." The conclusion to his thought was:

"And we felt sorry for . . . them? How naive can we be?"

Bruno Buti

CHAPTER 5

Heeding their guests' advice, the Italians spent the following day studying the river and in so doing, decided to make the crossing the next day. The water had receded somewhat, but then, there was the question of quicksand. Giving thought to the matter and knowing their animals' keen sense of self-preservation and their inclination not to panic under adverse conditions, they decided to trust their instinct and let the oxen pick the course. Obviously, precautions would be taken to lessen the risk of losing even one of their prized oxen to quicksand. Therefore, since it was late afternoon, again, they'd stay camped for the night and attempt the crossing in the morning.

When word got to the Wagon Master of the Italians' plans, he was infuriated. Turning to his equally drunken buddy, the ferry tender, he swore:

"Damned ya Jason! Why'n ya tell me there was shallow water downstream! Now look what ya went'n done! Ya let them dang Dagos git ahead of us'n!"

"Ya jest hold it a dang'd minute, ya damned foul-mouthed critter!" retaliated Jason while staggering to his feet.

"I didn't tell ya then because the river was high, and that shallow water is still plum full of pockets of quicksand regardless!"

"The hell ya say!" snorted Harvey, the now impressed, but drunken, Wagon Master.

"Wa'll thets jest fine, jest fine, let 'em try it. Only an injun can pick his way through thet thar quicksand, an they's not injuns, thet's fer sure!"

Dago Red! Westward - Ho!

Gleefully, the Wagon Master rose to his feet, took a long pull of firewater before firmly addressing Elder Jeb who had brought him the great news. In his slobbering drunken manner, he ordered:

"Jeb, ya see to it thet no damned Red Skin gits near thems dang Dagos. Scalp 'em if'n ya have to!"

Following the order, he grinned with delight.

"Quicksand, by Gawd, thet'll slow 'em down! They's about to learn what the West is all about!"

In a drunken slur, Jason remarked:

"Harvey, you're a slimy snake if I ever saw one!"

Come daylight next morning, as campfire smoke hung over the main group's camp, bacon sizzling in fry pans while coffee pots perked, the elders stood around watching the Italians in the camp downstream making preparations for the treacherous crossing. The Wagon Master and the ferry tender, drunker than victorious gladiators at a Roman orgy, didn't bother to pick themselves up off the ground to witness the event, for they were thoroughly convinced of its disastrous outcome.

Elder Jeb did the talking as the others watched and listened to his thoughtful comments:

"Now look at that. They've harnessed up that pair of oxen side by side over yonder at the water's edge, but they're not hooking them up to the wagon! Instead they've got the end of that laid out rope tied to the doubletree. I don't get it."

Glancing over to his left he now commented about the three pair of oxen as a team of six, harnessed up in a series of doubletrees, tied to the other end of the sturdy rope.

"Now this I've got to see," he said as the handler of the pair shed his clothing and, along with the pair of oxen, dipped into the slow current of the river.

Moving along cautiously up to his armpits, staying upstream from the animals and hanging on to their harness, kept up a calm conversation with his charges. Slowly they moved along, feeling their way as the handler of the six oxen team on firm ground, likewise talking to his charges, kept the rope taught while backing up at the same pace as the pair now belly deep fording the river.

"Well I'll be damned!" exclaimed Elder Jeb. Then horrified, exclaimed:

"Oh my God! Quicksand!"

Suddenly, a third of the way into the stream, the oxen's front quarters dipped below water line. A command signal from their handler to his colleague on shore instantly put the six team oxen, now pulling forward, straining to the task of backing their counterparts out of the sucking action of the quicksand pothole they'd stepped into.

Amongst exclamations, groans and moans, men of the main group, now joined by women and children, moved in closer as they recited prayers aloud. The Italians, men, women and children alike, also looked on in horror. As the rope stretched to the stiffness of steel, the men knowing the weak point to be at the knotted ends, instantly split into two groups, one to take hold of the rope at the end tied to the six team doubletree and the other scrambling into the river to relieve the pressure at that end, lest the rope shear itself at the knot.

Seeing the purpose of the maneuver, Elder Jeb yelled out to his group in despair:

"Men!" he commanded, "they need help! Come on, let's get over there and lend a hand!"

Further instruction was not needed for they all well knew what had to be done. Within an instant the length of rope between the two doubletrees, both in and out of the water, was encased in calloused, powerful hands. As many as there was room for, in the river itself, strained at the doubletree to relieve the strain on the rope.

Dago Red! Westward - Ho!

Young John, staying with his mount, plunged the animal into the river, uncoiled his lariat, tossed one end to the closest man to the submerged doubletree and shouted an order as he flipped the other end into a half-hitch around the saddle horn:

"Get it on the crossbeam! Cinch it tight!"

No easy task while groping around underwater, but nevertheless the deed was done. Surging back onto firm ground, John added his horse's strength to the effort.

Prayers from the lips of those who could not offer physical help rose above the commands and urgings emitting from the lips of the men on the line. Holding on to the harness, the handler of the periled oxen stayed with his animals, constantly assuring them that they'd be rescued. At his urging, rather than thrash around in panic that would cause them to sink deeper into the sand pocket, they remained calm, holding their breath as instinct dictated, thus adding buoyancy to overcome their massive weight.

At the urging of the handler on shore, the six oxen applied their awesome strength to the task. Leaning heavily into it, muscles reflecting the effort, trenching the ground as hooves dug in for traction, coupled with men synchronously tugging on the rope for its entire length, they defied the awesome grip of nature's sucking action associated with quicksand. A sudden surge of water swirling into the cavity made by the two threatened oxen as they were dragged backwards onto firm footing signaled success. Exhaling a blast of foul air as their snouts rose above the surface brought about a joyous shout from the spectators, first the women and children, then followed by excited exclamations amongst the men, back slapping, hand shaking, and congratulations acting as if having just won a tug-o-war at a county fair. The fact that they were of completely different ethnic background made no difference. Praying along with the rest, Reverend Gadwall slapped shut the Bible he'd been reading from with a final comment:

"Lord, thank you for showing us the way. Amen!"

As much excitement as there was, Giuseppina could not turn her attention away from John. The deed, his manner of handling the horse, was not the entire attraction. Her previous encounter had already sparked a flame within her that intensified with his every move. She couldn't hide her flushed expression, at least not to her father. He wondered.

However, the joyous reveling suddenly simmered down to a low murmur as someone pointed out the phenomenon taking place in the river just ahead of the two oxen now standing in water lapping up under their bellies, while being caressed by their handler. The many bodies in the water tugging on the rope, the oxen themselves, the activity having disrupted the normal flow of water, the shifting current stirring up the treacherous sand pit, had created a swirling whirlpool effect outlining the boundaries of the quicksand pocket. The size of it could have easily swallowed up a team of horses, covered wagon and all. The disrupted current divulged another such pocket downstream. The chilling thought of the consequences of being caught up and sucked into one of these pockets was quite sobering, to say the least.

Now that they knew how to identify these pockets of quicksand, men and boys scurried up and down the banks of the river in hopes of learning more about this quicksand phenomenon. They reported back that apparently there were a series of such pockets downstream, whereas there was no sign of any upstream. Talking it over, ignoring the pleas to the contrary by the womenfolks, it was decided to try the fording of the river again. The handler now guided his oxen further upstream, but once on the move again, and now also knowing what they were dealing with, the oxen, following their own instincts, carefully feeling their way along the bottom and eyeing the action of the current up ahead, skirted the quicksand pocket and, with their handler at their side, emerged from the water on the opposite side, safe and sound.

Again, the whooping and hollering echoed off the surrounding bluffs. While those on the opposite side reveled, the handler guided the oxen some ten paces upstream where he then tied the rope fast to a sturdy tree. Waving the all clear to the men on the opposite side, they in turn followed the procedure. In a no nonsense activity, oxen were immediately backed up to wagons. Shouting instructions to each other, the Italians lined up their wagons and proceeded to ford the river using the rope as a guide. As he was ready to leave, Capo Giuseppe approached Elder Jeb with extended hand, and in his best fashion thanked him and others gathered around for their help, and wished them well. But Elder Jeb, holding firmly to Capo Giuseppe's hand, asked of his new friend:

"Will you leave the rope tied up long enough so we can follow you across?' he asked. "It won't take us long to get hitched up," he added, then said, "I'll be the last one to leave and will then untie the rope on this end."

The answer came forth with a broad grin and firm shake of the hand:

"Yes, and we'll not leave until you are safely across."

Soaked from the waist down, John retrieved his lariat, tied it back on the saddle strappings and, as he reined his equally wet horse, glanced over his shoulder in hopes of getting a glimpse of Giuseppina. She was there, watching his every move with admiration. His yearning stare was met with a pleasant, beckoning expression, the warmth of their glances melting the ethnic barrier between them. The thought and hope that they'd meet again stimulated their yearning for each other.

By the time the bell wagon, the last in line, dipped into the river, schooners from the main group were lining up to follow. As they were getting into position, one of the mule skinners ran up to Elder Jeb, now astride his saddle supervising, ready to take up the rear.

"Jeb, how about the Wagon Master? What are we going to do about him? He's lay'n over there out cold, maybe dead!"

A reasonable assumption considering he'd ingested enough spiked alcohol to embalm an elephant.

"Damn him and that drunken friend of his," answered Jeb in disgust.

"I guess we best not leave him."

Thinking for an instant, he ordered:

"Go fetch his damned horse. Saddle him up and bring him here...pronto!"

The order was obeyed; the horse was ready for a rider.

"Give me the reins, fetch a couple of men and come with me!" he again ordered, then trotted his horse over to the Wagon Master. Dropping the reins of both horses as he dismounted, it wasn't more than a minute before the mule skinner along with two other men came running up while asking a question:

"What ya planning to do Jeb? He ain't fit to set in a saddle."

"We ain't going to set him in the saddle! We're going to drape him over the saddle and tie him down! Come on, give me a hand!" And so the deed was done.

Jeb swung into his saddle as he issued a final order:

"Hand me the reins! Now get going, we're wasting time! I'll take up the rear, drag him across if I have to!"

"Better keep an eye on him, he's liable to drown hanging like that!" warned Jake, the mule skinner, as they parted. In a low murmur Jeb responded:

"Serve him right if he does!"

No sooner had the last schooner reached the opposite

shore, Elder Jeb, now mounted, untied the rope and with the Wagon Master's horse in tow spurred his own horse into the swirling waters. On occasion the Wagon Master's head, in it's hanging position, dipped under the surface, the chilling effect bringing the Wagon Master somewhat back to his senses. Coughing and sputtering profanity, he swore he'd shoot the lot of them for their actions. But having anticipated as much, Elder Jeb had the Wagon Master's gun belt strung around his shoulders with no intention of giving it back until the man was fully sober.

Once on shore the Wagon Master was untied, eased off his horse, and held upright until equilibrium was established. Not until then did he realize that they were not standing on the opposite shore. He barked:

"How'n hell'd we git here? Whose idea was it cross'n agin orders? Ah'm in charge here! Speak up or ah'll . . ." with that, he swung his arm down expecting to palm his six shooter but to his displeasure, it was in Elder Jeb's possession.

"Gimme ma gun!" he demanded.

"You'll get it back when you calm down!" responded Elder Jeb. Then added:

"The Italians got us across, and by God there ain't going to be no shoot'n damn it!"

"I-tal-ians!" he exclaimed in anger.

"Them's dang little Dagos, ah'll . . ."

Without finishing the explosive threat, a sudden change of expression from anger to horror crossed what could be seen of his bearded face. The enormous concentration of jalapeño pepper juice used to spike the rotgut whiskey he'd ingested had by now activated an overwhelming fermentation process within his innards that within a matter of minutes, unless immediately relieved, would reach explosive proportions. Breaking away in short but fast steps, butt muscles tensed up restraining nature's call, unbuckling his belt as he trotted along, he made a beeline for the willow rushes at the river's edge.

The moans and groans that followed shortly after attested to the agony of ridding himself of the red hot concoction simmering within his innards like a volcanic caldera. The surging burning feeling in the course of defecation could be likened to his having a cattle rustler's red hot running iron being rammed up his ass. Fearing that he may not have survived the ordeal, upon investigating his long absence, the Wagon Master was found sitting in hip deep water with no desire to remove himself from its cooling effect.

Followed by several of the elders, Elder Jeb approached the Italians as they were preparing to depart. Apologetically he said:

"Again, we apologize for the conduct of the Wagon Master, and we want you to know that we are your friends. Please reconsider and travel with us."

With his own people gathered around him, old Giuseppe, in his best manner, answered:

"No. It is best that we move on. To remain among you, with your friend the Wagon Master's feeling towards us being such as it is, will only make trouble for you as well as ourselves. We have dealt with bullies before, and have no desire to do so again."

"I understand your feelings. But the Wagon Master is not our friend. He is only a guide employed by the government. Nothing more. But go if you must. We will remain here for the rest of the day and possibly tomorrow as well. This will give you a good head start. Hopefully when we meet again, the Wagon Master by then will show more respect for you and your people," stated Elder Jeb as he extended his hand for a handshake, then added:

"May God be with you."

"And with you as well," came the farewell response.

Dago Red! Westward - Ho!

CHAPTER 6

The Italians, now well ahead of their counterparts, followed the beaten path, once again picking up the North Platte River and following it along past Scotts Bluff. Stopping off at Fort Laramie long enough to verify that they were still on course, they moved on past Horeshoe Station, then on to Laperelle Station where they were advised that the North Platte River which they must ford up ahead apiece was running quite high due to thunderstorms in the mountains beyond. Sure enough, upon reaching the crossing they found this to be true. So they set up camp to wait out the high water and, in the meantime, replenish their meat supply.

While the grownups busied themselves with their chores, the teens (boys), using braided horsehair snares, caught small game and birds which were preserved in barrels of salt along with other meats, the needed ingredients for making pasta and polenta sauces. The women busied themselves with household chores as well as gathering up herbs of various sorts, again to spice up and flavor the sauces. And of course, set about baking sourdough bread. The aroma of the freshly baked bread wafted downwind of the camp, catching the attention of a band of hungry rag-tag Indians who were also camped along the river.

Their habitat having been overrun and abused by the White Man, as well as their main source of meat, the buffalo, slaughtered to near extinction, and uprooted as a community, rather than starve and at the risk of being mutilated as in the past, they approached the Italian encampment cautiously in hopes of getting a handout. To their surprise, instead of being mistreated and scalped at the hands of the White Man as they were now becoming accustomed, they were received as guests. Since hand gestures and expressions along with uttered sounds was a custom for both parties, communication barriers were soon hurdled.

The amazing part of this encounter, due to the similarity in communication, certainly not becoming to the White Man, feathered hats the men wore along with colorful attire, although of different design, and their dance, "La Tarantella," much like their own, along with the sharing of food, a custom amongst visiting tribes, led them to believe that these people were in fact not the same as the White Man they'd known.

As with the Indians, the Italians' diet included small game, birds and just about anything and everything that swam, crawled or flew, however prepared in a different manner, sauce, for corn meal (polenta), and thought to be earth worms (spaghetti). But most impressive, they drank what was first thought to be ox blood until explained that it was not but rather, "vino," the nectar of life, a sexual stimulant, that made them feel good and rejuvenated. Once having ingested a fair ration of this so-called "vino," and now feeling better, they truly believed their hosts to be their Saviors.

The huge bell, believed to be a cannon of tremendous destructive power, therefore an awesome secret weapon, strengthened their respect for their hosts. They'd make no trouble for them, but rather they'd share their knowledge of the vast expanse that lie ahead that must be traversed. They also warned their hosts that their Indian counterparts had a hatred for the White Man and, if possible, they should play down any resemblance to them lest they'd be met with extreme violence.

In the two days of encampment, the bond between this destitute remnant of a once-proud Indian tribe and the Italians grew strong, thus the Indians volunteered to guide their newly made friends in the crossing of the treacherous river. Even though it had receded to a respectable level, it was nevertheless tricky to negotiate the rough, boulder-strewn bottom at the head of the roaring rapids, the only place the crossing could safely be made.

On the third day as preparations were in progress, the Indians, ears to the ground, reported a caravan of schooners approaching from the east. In panicked fear their Chief, "No Horse" (so named because he could never afford a horse), exclaimed:

"White Man come! We must leave at once!"

"Leave . . . why?" asked Capo Giuseppe.

"White Man kill! Scalp! Maybe you too!"

"They will not do that. We know these people, they're our friends!" assured the Capo. But the Indians were not convinced.

"Maybe not your people, but my people, yes!" assured the Chief, then added:

"Government man called "Harvey," him with your friends? Him bad medicine, evil man! Better you come with us! You look much like Indian!"

Suddenly a flashback crossed Capo Giuseppe's mind: The swatches of hair dangling from the Wagon Master's saddle were Indian scalps! He was stunned by the horrifying thought that this man, their tormentor, was indeed a killer, to say the least, a dangerous man. Judging by his actions and feelings towards themselves, a possible psychopath or just a plain killer for profit, either way a threat to whomever he took a disliking to, and he most certainly had demonstrated his dislike for the Italians. And now, having befriended the Indians who he preyed upon for the value of their scalps, Lord only knows the carnage that could take place if they, the Italians, were found to be fraternizing with this band of Indians.

Giving real thought to their predicament, Capo Giuseppe answered with a firm:

"Yes! The man's name is Harvey." Then asked:
"Give me but a few moments to talk to my people before you leave?"

"Make it quick!" responded Chief No Horse.

Already gathered around, the heads of these diverse families, immigrant clans from Italy, Toscani, Piedmontesi, Romani, Siciliani and others, were apprized of the situation. When asked, they unanimously agreed to move out with the Indians.

"Will you guide us across the river?' asked Capo Giuseppe of the Chief.

"Yes, we ride wagons with you, show the way!"

In short order camp was broken and oxen harnessed. Once out in midstream it became obvious that if it were not for the Indians' knowledge of the river, a disastrous outcome would be eminent. The deafening roar of the rapids downstream in itself was chilling. On the other hand, the Indians were impressed by the oxen handlers' courage and consideration towards their animals as they stayed with them in water up to their armpits.

By the time the last of the wagons emerged from the turbulent waters, the main group with Wagon Master Harvey astride his horse, appeared at the water's edge on the opposite side. Reining his steed up tight in anger at the sight of the Italians on the opposite side of the river, not only still ahead of him but now fraternizing with Indians, whether they were Pawnee, Cheyenne or Ute, good or bad, made no difference to him. He'd kill them all and scalp them, Italians included if they dared intervene.

The plan had been for the main group to camp overnight on the east side of the Platte as the Italians had, give their animals a rest, and allow the river to recede for a safer crossing. But now the Wagon Master had second thoughts. There for the taking, just across the river, was a small fortune in

Dago Red! Westward - Ho!

scalps. The Indians were sitting ducks. Aside from a few rag-tag braves with make-shift spears, bows and arrows, all that stood between him and them was a group of short statured men carrying walking staffs, and a river to cross. As Wagon Master, if he played his cards right, using his charges to an advantage, staying in close to the lead wagon until once onto dry land, whereby he'd spur his horse on past the unsuspecting Italians, catch the Indians off guard and slaughter them mercilessly. Reining his horse up alongside Elder Jeb's horse, as Jeb was about to guide the lead wagon, his own, into camp formation, Harvey demandingly issued new instructions:

"Jeb, we ain't goin' ta camp on this side! We uns'll cross over and make camp on tuther side!" The order was questioned.

"Harvey, it doesn't make sense. Why not camp here tonight and cross tomorrow morning? The water will be lower, easier to cross. Besides, these animals have been pushed hard all day. They need a rest.'

"I don't give a dang 'bout the animals! We cross now!"

Elder Jeb was set back. He now saw something in this man that was frightening. He studied him carefully, wondering about the Indian scalps he always seemed to have an abundance of, the blood-encrusted, long blade knife held firmly in its leather scabbard with rawhide, no doubt used for scalping. And now, sitting astride his saddle with palm resting on the butt of his gun as if ready to jerk it out of his holster, loaded Winchester in its saddle scabbard, his pale blue, steel-cold eyes had the fierce look of a snake ready to strike. The Wagon Master in a chilling snarl repeated his order:

"Ya hear'd what ah say'd! Pass the word on down the line! Then ya climb up on yer wagon an take the reins! Ah'l take yer hoss with me!"

At this point, Elder Jeb felt it best to comply.

Seeing his dad hand the reins to Harvey then climb up on the lead wagon, John came trotting up alongside with a puzzled question:

"What gives? Why'd he take your horse?"

"We're crossing over now. That's the order."

"What the hell! That's stupid!"

"Son, calm down! We'll do as he says . . . for now!"

It was a cunning plan. By taking Jeb's horse with him, Jeb struggling midstream with his wagon, the Wagon Master, well ahead, surging forward, releasing Jeb's horse on the opposite bank and now, with no one to interfere could carry out his murderous plot: slaughter the Indians, and if the Italians intervene, shoot them as well.

The Indian Chief, having recognized the Wagon Master from times past, first moved his people back away from the riverbank, then seriously fearful, came back to warn his newly made friend, Capo Giuseppe:

"This is him! The bad man!" he stated while eyeing the Wagon Master's movement from across the river.

"There is no need to worry," responded Capo Giuseppe. "They will camp there for the night. That will give you much time to move your people away from here."

"No, my friend! You are wrong! The bad one will trick us! He will come across now, pretending to be a friend. Then like a snake hypnotizing its prey . . . strike!!"

Together, those two wise old men of different ethnic backgrounds, entrusted to watch over their people, studied the movements across the river with interest. Schooner after schooner appeared on the scene, but they were not being guided into a camping formation as might be expected, but rather, being kept in line in preparation for the fording of the river. It now became obvious to Capo Giuseppe that the Indian Chief was right.

"My friend," said Capo Giuseppe thoughtfully, "you are

right!" They will be coming . . . we must prepare to deal with the Wagon Master!"

"This is not your problem! This is our problem! It is our scalps that he wants!" said the Chief firmly.

"Maybe that is so, but we too must someday have to deal harshly with this abusive bully, and I think the time is now! Yes! This is a good time! While he has scalping on his mind, we will catch him off guard!"

"How? You have no guns except the cannon. And one shot will kill many of your friends as well!"

The comment about the cannon drew raised eyebrows and a shrug of shoulders from the heads of the clans as they, too, had by now joined the two leaders in observing the activities across the river. In their native tongue, they discussed the matter of the Indian's misunderstanding of the purpose of the bell. However, also in his native tongue, Capo Giuseppe responded to their comments:

"Let it be. We have a much more serious matter to deal with."

Now turning back to the Chief, he said:

"Keep your people back and directly behind us. If the bad one intends to do what you say, he'll have to pass through us first! We will deal with him, that I will assure you!" he stated with expressed confidence, then added:

"Go now! They are starting to cross!"

The Chief, impressed with the Italian's determination, parted to carry out the order while the heads of the Italian clans huddled around wise old Giuseppe to formulate the plan of deterring the Wagon Master from carrying out his assumed plot, to scalp their newly made friends, the Indians, and maybe bring harm to themselves in the process.

The Wagon Master in the lead, with Elder Jeb's horse in tow, picked his way through the swirling waters while directing Jeb at the reins of the lead schooner. They were doing fine in spite of the fact that the deafening roar of the rapids below all but made verbal conversation next to impossible. Other schooners and freight wagons dipped into the waters, one behind the other. The Italian heads of their respective clans, standing abreast forming two lines, one several yards behind the other, putting up a front, smiling, chattering encouragement, waited at the water's edge.

Once the lead schooner passed midpoint, the Wagon Master made his move. Spurring his horse, he broke away from the caravan. Surging through the swift current, both mounted steed and empty-saddled horse in tow, at the commands of the Wagon Master pushed hard toward shore where the cheering Italians waited. As they were approached, the horse in tow was released to fend for itself. The hand that held the reins dropped to the butt of the six-shooter, retrieving it in a firm grip. There was no question now in the minds of the Italians that the Indian was right! The intent was clear.

With the roar of the rapids still well pronounced, Elder Jeb on the lead wagon swore:

"No! You damned son-of-a-bitch! Damn you, Harvey! So that's your game!" Following that exclamation, he yelled to his team as he cracked his whip over their heads and slapped the reins on their backs:

"Ya! Ya! Damn it! Ya! Ya! Giddy up! Go! Damned ya, go!"

Frenzied, the team lurched forward, with the sudden jarring action breaking the strappings holding the piano in place. Free of its bounds, the heavy piano rolled back, demolishing the tailgate as it tumbled into the fast current. Not bothering to concern himself with the loss of his precious cargo, Elder Jeb, now standing, continued to push his team for all it could bear. The thought of knowing that the Wagon Master had, in fact, tricked him, especially for such an evil purpose, was driving him to near destruction.

However, the real destruction was now taking place in the rapids. The piano, tumbling end for end, crashing

Dago Red! Westward - Ho!

against outcroppings of boulders, banging up against stumps and brushing against jagged snags as it rode the turbulent foaming rapids, was hammering out a crescendo of garbled music echoing off the crags above, the likes of which only an enraged madman pounding out his own funeral march could have composed. The "Grand Finale" was punctuated by the combined explosion of all the keys simultaneously as the piano hit the pool at the bottom of the waterfall to its total disintegration.

Reverend Gadwall, giving no thought to the fact that his pony was several hands shorter in height than the horses, upon reaching midstream, although firmly draped over the saddle, was up to his armpits in water while, with the exception of the pony's snout, the animal was completely submerged and being held to firm footing by the sheer weight of his rider. Astounded at the utterances in berating Mister Harvey, Reverend Gadwall denounced his fellow clergyman, Elder Jeb, by firmly stating: "Good Lord... Elder Jeb! Your choice of words...? Not very becoming for a man of the cloth! I suggest you promptly repent lest ye face the wrath of God!"

As the words were spoken, his short legged pony dropped into a pot hole thus in a thrashing swirl of the turbulant water, with the exception of the reverends hat, the whole of this configuration disappeared below the surface .

On shore the Wagon Master reined his galloping steed into the midst of the Italians, screaming:

"Get the hell outta the way, ya damned bunch of Dagos!"

The Italians, whose smiles had now given way to warrior-like expressions, descendants of Roman Gladiators and warriors with the art of self-defense and the strategy of unity in taking the offensive in battle against overwhelming odds bred into them, as the raving maniac, gun in hand, came charging through, now having changed their position to running alongside the horse, and from both sides, tossed their staffs horizontally between the flailing legs of the galloping, frenzied horse, thus bringing his hammering hooves to an abrupt halt.

Crashing to the ground, the rider catapulted out of the saddle and reacting to instinct, fired his pistol sending its projectile harmlessly crashing through the canopy of the cottonwoods bordering the river. He was yet to stop tumbling through the dust when a sharp blow from a staff crushed the knuckles of his gun hand, thus sending the gun tumbling out of reach. But, this man, a vicious, seasoned fighter in his own right, bounced up on his feet with knife in hand, held in a manner to gut the first man who dared come near him. With the speed and accuracy of a leopard's paw, the staff in the hands of an Alpine Mountaineer, a Lombardese, smashed the knife hand as he had Harvey's gun hand.

As quick as a cheetah bringing down an impala, Capo Giuseppe stepped in, flipped the garrote around the stunned Wagon Master's neck, thus pulling him to the ground, rendering him helpless and gasping for breath. Others quickly moved in. The garroter keeping a tight grip, they dragged their victim to the closest cottonwood tree. Standing him back on his feet, while being held firmly by both arms and legs, the Sicilian among them picked up the victim's knife, ran his thumb over its edge to verify its sharpness, and in a no-nonsense manner strode up to the now bewildered, wide-eyed, gasping bully, commanded old Giuseppe, the garroter, to loosen his grip lest the man die before he'd have the opportunity to learn some manners, said:

"So, you like the word "Dago!" Well, let us see how you like the word 'liver!' Your liver!" With that, a quick slice of the knife cut through Harvey's clothing.

The Indians, having moved up closer, were astounded

at the event that was taking place right before their eyes. Such tactics in subduing a well-armed aggressor were something they'd never witnessed before. And the punishment he was about to receive, by what they could surmise, left them to wonder, just where did these people come from? Why are they here?

Elder Jeb, with the pounding music of his demolished piano still ringing in his ears, having leaped off his schooner as it reached shallow water, came sloshing up at a fast pace while calling out to the victors in frenzied pleadings:

"For God's sake, no! Don't! That is not the way! We are not Barbarians! In the name of Jesus Christ!! Stop!"

Hearing the name of the Holy Savior coming from Elder Jeb's frenzied lips, although not of the Catholic faith but unquestionably a Christian, caused the Sicilian to momentarily abort his intended mission, to slice open the belly of the now trembling heathen, pleading for his life through quivering lips.

Elder Jeb, running up to the knife wielder, breathing hard from his ordeal, once again pleaded:

"Listen to me! He is not worth the trouble this . . . this . . . whatever it is you intend to do . . . it will cause you much trouble!"

Chief No Horse now standing directly behind Elder Jeb, listened attentively to the Sicilian's stern response as he held the knife firmly at ready. In heavy accented English he said:

"We left the Old Country, and suffered extreme hardships in doing so, just to get away from tyranny, cowardly bullies, men of this character, heathens! Never again shall we tolerate such abusive conduct from cockroaches the likes of this man! Yes, my friend, as you wish! We'll spare his life...this time!"

To the horror of the bystanders, as swift as a bolt of lightening and with the accuracy and skill of a surgeon, the knife slashed across the forehead of the horrified Wagon Master just deep enough to cause blood to ooze and flow down across his fear-paled face, thoroughly saturating his shaggy mustache, seeping past his quivering lips and into his gaping mouth. While gagging on his own blood, the order was given to release him. Although free to move away, he remained rigidly with his back to the cottonwood tree as the interpretation of the Sicilian's gesture and final comment sank into his twisted brain.

As the words were spoken:

"The next time!" the Sicilian ran the back edge of the knife first across his own throat, then across his forehead, the act to be interpreted as:

"First, your throat! Then your scalp!"

CHAPTER 7

Chief No Horse was quite impressed by the tactics used to subdue their tormentor, the Wagon Master, and more so their being accepted as equals by their newly-made friends and hosts, the Italians. In a no-nonsense manner, the Chief asked for Harvey's knife. Having been given the knife, cradling it in the palm of his hand and with motions of hand and spoken words, stated:

"The blood encrusted on the handle of this knife is the blood of my people. The fresh blood on the blade is the blood of the man that put it there, our tormentor, the man called Harvey."

Then addressing the Italians directly, stated:

"Thanks to you, my friends, our sufferings have been vindicated. We are grateful."

The Chief then asked if he could keep the knife. There appearing to be no objection, he made an impressive commitment:

"This knife shall remain as is, the blood never removed, to be kept but never again used for its intended purpose but rather as a reminder of the injustices of scalping."

It was now apparent that these Indians were not scroungy beggars as first thought, but rather a proud and understanding splinter of the Cheyenne tribe forced into their predicament by the stupid policies of government politicians in Washington who cared not to soil their polished boots in taking to the fields to oversee the activity of the idiots they'd assigned to supposedly administer fairness and justice to these Native Americans.

Although never having been threatened by the pioneers who made up the main caravan, many of whom had yet to make it across the river, Chief No Horse was taking no chances. Speaking for his people, he bade their benefactors "goodbye," retreated from the scene of turmoil, and as if evaporating in thin air, vanished into the wilderness leaving the Italians wondering: would they ever see them or their kind ever again?

After seeing to it that the Wagon Master was attended to, Elder Jeb now having taken full command of the caravan passed the word down the line that they would make camp and remain for at least another day. This was a welcomed relief after the grueling pace set by the Wagon Master. Aside from the loss of the piano, the horse-drawn wagons had little problem making it across. But not so with the mules; they balked. There was no way that they'd plunge into the raging current of the rain swollen river. The massive, sensitive ears tuned into the macabre orchestrated shock waves emitting from the piano in its final death throes had them at the brink of stampeding. So since it had been decided to stay over another day, Jake the mule skinner chose to make camp on the east side of the river, calm his mules down and wait for better conditions.

Elder Jeb now ordered his son, John, who'd also waded the river on horseback, his own saddle horse having spooked at the sudden burst of the horrendously loud garbled music along with the blasting report of the gun, thrashing in a macabre dance, in a sloshing frenzy, having been released hightailed it for parts unknown, to retrieve his horse and the Wagon Master's, which had apparently suffered no serious injury when tripped, but in the confusion that ensued, picked himself up and trotted off.

As for Reverend Gadwall, having been swept out of the saddle by the turbulent waters, of which had it not occurred,

Dago Red! Westward - Ho!

his pony would have drowned for sure, and had it not been for his tight death-like grip on the reins, and his gas bloated torso that kept him afloat, and the pony's determination to save his own hide by swimming furiously toward shore while towing his buoyant blubber-laden cargo, the reverend would have suffered the same fate as the piano. Once at the shore, exhausted as he was, the pony pulling backwards dragged the sputtering reverend up onto dry land. In his soaked, nearly drowned condition, in an oratorical, garbled barrage, he let fly a blast of profanity directed at his panting, water-logged pony. With a final clear cut opinion of the animal's behavior, he stated:

"You stupid-damned-son-of-a-heathen-whore! If it were not for God's intervention, you'd have had me drowned! Be assured, that, the Good Lord knows of your cursed ways!"

If in fact God did intervene, it could be assumed that his concentration was to favor the pony for in the violent, frenzied shake of hide, the animal not only rid himself of water, but also shed himself of the reverend's water soaked belongings.

The Italians, their tranquil way of life having been disrupted, expressed their regrets to Elder Jeb and to those who had by now joined him, and in so doing let it be known that they'd be moving on. By then the last of the horse-drawn wagons had made it across, only to be followed by a regiment of Mounted Cavalry on a mission heading south to Fort Bridger.

Having been riding hard since they'd left Fort Laramie, it was a welcome relief to dismount and mingle with the gathering of people. Encouraged to unsaddle their horses, helping hands assisted in rubbing down the sweaty animals. The Italians, in a better position to do so, offered snacks to the dusty, fatigued soldiers. Although not too sure of what they were eating or what was being said by the Italian women serving, they nevertheless enjoyed the offerings.

Shortly, John, the elder's son who had been assigned to retrieve the two runaway saddle horses, came trotting in with his father's and the Wagon Master's horses in tow. Stopping short of the main crowd, a curious soldier walked up taking note of the Wagon Master's saddle with its scabbarded Winchester, But it wasn't the rifle that interested him, it was the Indian scalps dangling from their leather bindings that had caught his eye. Examining each one carefully, he then took the reins in hand and walked the horse over to the Colonel in command and interrupted his conversation with Elder Jeb.

"Sir," said the soldier as he snapped a salute, "you might want to take a look at this . . . , Sir."

"Why? What did you find?"

"Indian scalps . . ., Sir."

"Indian scalps! You sure?" questioned the Colonel as he turned to fully face the soldier.

"Yes Sir, I'm sure. Take a look."

The Colonel strode up to the saddle and examined the hairy pelts, as did the soldier, then exclaimed firmly:

"What the hell! Whose horse is this?" he demanded to know.

Elder Jeb stepped up to explain the reason for a riderless horse but was cut short.

"Is this animal yours?"

"No Sir. My horse is that one over yonder," pointing to the horse being held by the lad still mounted on his own.

"That's right . . . Sir. This is my dad's horse," attested the lad.

"Damn it!" swore the Colonel. "I don't give a damn about that horse! This one . . . right here! Who the hell's horse is it?"

Seeing no point in trying to explain much of anything, Elder Jeb pointed to the Wagon Master sitting in a resting position up against a wagon wheel. The bloodied bandage about his forehead giving credence to his reason for not

Dago Red! Westward - Ho!

standing, the question was answered:

"The horse belongs to Mister Harvey, our Wagon Master."

Marching stiff legged up to Harvey, the Colonel, ignoring his condition, asked three consecutive questions as sharp as the report of a rifle:

"That your horse? Those scalps yours? Did you take them?"

Struggling to get to his feet, once erect the Wagon Master barely audible, stated :

"I'm an Official Government Agent, a Guide . . . Sir."

"I don't give a good God-damned who the hell you are . . . Mister!" barked the Colonel. "And damned if I'll ask you again! Sargent! Take this man into custody! Get him on his horse! We'll take him into Fort Bridger," he commanded.

"Damned filthy murderer, bushwhacker! How the hell can we ever expect to keep the peace out here by scalping Indians?" he growled as he moved through the gathered crowd. He again commanded:

"Saddle up! We're moving out, pronto!"

Elder Jeb, somewhat worried about the Wagon Master's ability to sustain a three-day ride in his present condition, stated:

"Sir, if I may. Mister Harvey has a bad gash across his forehead."

"How'd he get it?" asked the Colonel, now somewhat calmer.

"Well, Sir, he had a confrontation with those people over there," answered Elder Jeb while pointing towards the Italians.

"There was this small band of Indians being threatened, they intervened, tried to protect them from Mister Harvey. I stepped in before . . ."

Turning away before Elder Jeb could finish and looking up at the now mounted Harvey, it was apparent to the Colonel that the Wagon Master had come within a whisker of getting himself scalped. Left hand gripping reins and saddle horn simultaneously, left foot in the stirrup, he remarked as he swung his lean body into the saddle:

"Next time, mind your own business! Don't intervene!"

59

Then, in a stern jaw set command directed to his men, he gave the order to move out.

Stiff and straight as statues and in neat formation, flag snapping in the breeze, the soldiers trotted their steeds out of sight. The Cavalry was on an important mission to back up the garrison at Fort Bridger while they in turn responded to the urgent matter of an atrocious massacre of emigrants having taken place days before somewhere south of Salt Lake City.

CHAPTER 8

Bidding their friends a final farewell, the Italians, now less joyful than they had been, followed the cavalry out. For John and Giuseppina, the parting was even less joyful. They barely had a chance to say "hello and goodby" before their parting of the ways. They held their eye contact to the very last. For the moment, that was all they had, but in their hearts felt that there'd be another time.

Surprisingly, considering the delayed start, they made it to Horse Creek, a small stream teaming with fish. There they camped for the night. As handlers tended their animals and other domestic stock, the women, teenage boys and girls delightfully waded into the stream with spaghetti colanders, pots and pans, scooping up brilliantly colored trout for the evening meal. By dusk skillets and frying pans over sagebrush fueled fires were sizzling, turning out trout fried until they rattled. Once again the Italians were back to their old selves, drinking wine, feasting, reveling and chattering.

But the reveling was interrupted by the children's announcement that a mysterious phenomenon was taking place in the skies near where they'd come from. All fell silent as the group followed the children to a clearing where they had been playing kickball. In the twilight of evening, looking to the Northeast, a long series of puffs of smoke drifted upwards from a distant plateau, clearly highlighted by the rays of the setting sun against the hue of the evening blue. This was a new experience for them, and so they watched intensely, wondering its purpose. They did agree that this was indeed the work of man, no doubt a means of communication. And the fact that to their knowledge there were only Indians to be found in the general area, they wondered: "Could this phenomenon have anything to do with Chief No Horse and his little band of Indians they'd befriended?" Although they had no way of knowing, it most certainly did.

Had they been able to interpret the message being sent via smoke signals, it would have read:

"Urgent message from Chief No Horse to cousin, Chief Many Horse (so named because he'd cornered the cayuse market in the area), be advised, we have encountered a tribe of people of unknown origin now traveling westward. They are not Indian nor are they White Man, neither short nor tall, serve good food and life-giving nectar called "vino," are friendly, but vicious fighters when provoked. They possess a secret weapon, appears to be a huge cannon capable of firing multiple volleys of cannon balls at a time, much like Gatling gun only more deadly."

Due East of the plateau from yet another plateau a short burst of smoke puffs were seen to drift upward, an apparent response. The short return message read:

"Cousin No Horse, what the hell are you talking about? Will you repeat that?"

"All right, but pay attention. Communication rates are high."

"Reverse the charges. Let's have it!"

So the lengthy message was repeated, and a return message was soon received:

"Buffalo crap! I don't believe it! I'm from Missouri, you'll have to show me!"

"All right, if you don't believe me, go see for yourself. They'll soon be in the pass at Devil's Gate. Advise caution, do not display war paint!! Do not puncture barrels, they contain life-giving nectar, a strong sex stimulant that works fine on both squaw and buck!"

"Sex? The heck you say. I'll send out two of my best

scouts immediately to check it out."

And so Chief Many Horse assigned two of his best scouts to intercept the Italians, investigate the matter of the cannon and the vino, and report back their findings. With enough provisions (strips of jerky strung on a rawhide string) to last them several days, the scouts set out to carry out their mission to check out the awesome secret weapon and this supposed life-giving nectar, "vino."

At the break of day next morning, the Italians were once again on the move, trudging past Independence Rocks, so named for who knows what purpose, and entered Devil's Gate, rightfully named for the stretch ahead that narrowed down to nothing more than a rough, narrow, uphill stagecoach road that led over the pass, carved in a deep crevice with vertical slabs of granite extending forever upwards, giving the sensation of looking up from Hell. And as could be expected, when the worst of conditions are present, a team of six horses hitched to a stagecoach loaded with luggage and weary passengers came charging down from the opposite direction around a tight bend on a collision course with the Italian caravan. Needless to say, chaos ensued.

The driver with his fists full of reins leaned heavily back and screamed at the horses:

"Ho! Damned ya, ho!"

His partner riding shotgun alongside was as shocked as the driver, thus dropping the double barreled, rabbit-eared shotgun as he reached desperately for the brake. Gripping it firmly with both hands while leaning back like the driver, and at the top of his voice exclaimed:

"What the hell! Oh my God! Look out!"

The instant the words were spoken, the shotgun tumbled off the stagecoach causing the rabbit-eared hammers to strike the side of the coach thus setting off both barrels in a thunderous blast that echoed off the slabs of granite like the discharging of a thousand cannons. Thinking they were being attacked by a gang of notorious road agents, the startled passengers in a fit of panic soon found themselves piled atop each other from the sudden stop. Dazed, men struggled to crawl out from under a maze of skirts and petticoats as women screamed and thrashed over the unintentional hand groping that was taking place.

The two Indian scouts, having caught up to the Italian's slow moving caravan with its bell-bearing wagon creaking along following the barrel wagon, the bell's gaping mouth fully visible facing toward the rear like a cannon ready to discharge, and having left their horses out of sight, in quiet soft moccasined feet sneaked around boulders and stared in awe at the glistening bronze bell. From the way it was cradled, in their minds it was definitely a cannon of horrendous proportions.

As the creaking, groaning wagon disappeared around a bend, the booming double blast of the shotgun came echoing down the canyon, ricocheting from one granite slab to the other like the discharge of a thousand cannons. Fading in the distance like rolling thunder led the Indians to believe that they'd been discovered and that the horrendous, ear-splitting cannonade was meant for them. Startled and horrified, ignoring the matter of the barrel wagon, they hightailed it back from the canyon, leaped on their equally startled mounts, and needing no encouragement the frenzied horses galloped wide-eyed out of the canyon.

For the slow moving lead oxen taking the uphill climb at an even slower pace than normal, it was just a matter of taking one step less in order to come to a dead stop, and that's what they did the instant the frothing snouts of the fast moving lead horses appeared, racing around the bend. As for the horses, the sudden appearance of the white oxen blocking the entire narrow road had no choice but to come

Dago Red! Westward - Ho!

to an abrupt halt. Reacting simultaneously with the order to do so, hooves firmly planted to the ground is what brought about the severity of the calamity within the coach. The first to emerge from the dust engulfed coach was an indignant, enraged, tall, skinny woman clutching a parasol firmly in her right hand as she frantically struggled with the chore of reinstating her undergarments to their rightful position. The driver, having secured the reins, while cursing a blue streak dropped to the ground landing somewhat alongside the frustrated woman. He couldn't help but gawk at the aforementioned procedure. The struggling woman was not only skinny, but sinewy as well, not an ounce of fat on her. As for her breasts, a pair of fried eggs would fit the description quite well. Unusually attired in a black tailcoat over a white blouse, black hair pulled back tight from a sharp-nosed, thin narrow face and topped with a brimless, red-feather tufted, bright scarlet red hat, the whole of her appearance was indeed similar to a Downey Woodpecker. The woman stepped up to the driver and in a to-the-point, firm manner stated:

"I demand that you chastise that . . . that man . . . there!" she said pointing her parasol directly at the meek little banker crawling around on his hands and knees searching for his spectacles.

"Now, Ma'am, why should I do that? What'd he do?" questioned the driver.

Stepping up a little closer to the driver, she hammered him with a staccato of harsh words like a woodpecker driving an acorn into the thick bark of a cottonwood. Indignantly she said:

"He fondled me, had his face in my bloomers! That's what he done! Now do something about it!"

The situation already had his patience stretched to the limit, so sizing up his tormentor from head to toe, he snapped back:

"Lady, whatever the man done, I'm sure it was not intentional! At least it don't appear to have hurt you none!"

"Oh! The idea! You . . . you . . . look at you! You poor excuse for a man! Heinous fat ass!" she taunted.

"Damn it, lady!" shot back the driver, "All you got is a big mouth! You chicken lipped, snake, hipped, dried up hag!"

That was the ultimate insult. Before the driver could duck, he got whacked across the side of the head with the parasol.

The shouting and demands extended to others, all claiming to have lost something, if not their valuables, at least their dignity. But all they got from the driver was a dressing down and a fair ration of profanity.

By now the Italians, having gathered around assessing the situation, and of course witnessing the confrontation, talking among themselves couldn't help but wonder, who was the worst of the lot, the so-called White Man, or the Indians? So far, they'd had no trouble with the Indians, but a lot of trouble with the White Man. It was only a matter of minutes before they, too, were soon engaged in argument.

It was bad enough that there was no room to get passed each other, what with the granite slabs on the one side and a sheer embankment dropping off to a stream at the base of the granite slabs on the other, but now the pioneers with their schooners had caught up to their counterparts, the Italians, and therefore pulled up short behind the stalled bell wagon.

Mounted, Elder Jeb rode up alongside asking:

"What's the problem? Why the delay?"

But all he got was the shrugging of shoulders, an "I don't know" answer as he trotted his horse up the line. Reaching the lead end of the Italian caravan, the obvious became apparent. Needless to say, the Italians were happy to see him. As he dismounted they swarmed all over him. He was a Godsend, just the person they needed to argue their case.

As for his son John, also astride his trotting steed, reined up tight as he found what he was looking for, Giuseppina.

At the sight of him she flushed with excitement, as did her mother Maria sitting alongside, but for a different reason. She saw the flame of love flare up within the heart of her daughter, something they'd need to reckon with, and soon.

In the meantime, the mule train pulled up behind the horse drawn schooners thus firmly plugging up the canyon like pounding a cork in a wine bottle. Wondering what caused the hangup, Jake unharnessed a jackass from his team and riding him bareback, came trotting up to the chaotic scene. Both Jake and his jackass knew in an instant that this was a serious problem. The jackass, as smart if not smarter than the participants embroiled in this arm-waving free-for-all argument, ears rotating like huge antennae, took sides in the argument. Every time it was suggested that the late comers back out of the pass, he'd inhale to the point of bursting his lungs and let out a series of the most awesome braying blasts that echoed down the canyon like the wailing whistle of a runaway steam locomotive. Ears rotating like so many blooming sunflowers searching for the sun, his colleagues down at the end, both the jennies and jackasses, brayed back in support of Jake's jackass's argument, that in no way would the mules risk their lives for the likes of the stagecoach contingency.

The braying back and forth got so intense that it was a wonder that the vertical slabs of granite above didn't come cascading down upon the lot of them in an avalanche of destruction. And the more the participants argued, the more the mules brayed until finally the stagecoach driver threw his hat on the ground in disgust and defeat. But when he went to pick it up again, to his irritable dismay the jackass had his front hoof firmly implanted on it. The coach driver, having had no experience with mules, cursed the animal as he bent over, pulled up on the mule's fetlock while punching him in the rib cage with his fist, paying no heed to mule skinner Jake's warning:

"I wouldn't do that if I were you!"

Thus, in addition to the hoof print in his hat, he got the excruciatingly painful imprint from a set of mule teeth on his ass.

There was no question now as to who was going to do what. Smarting from the bite on the ass, and the "serves you right!" sarcastic, revengeful remark emitting from the puckered beak-like lips of the skinny woman passenger he'd chastised, the coach driver agreed to get turned around and head back where they'd come from, South Pass City at the head of the pass, the only place the stagecoach could go to get past the entire wagon train. Since they'd met at the midpoint of the long winding grade, it would take all of the rest of the day for the wagon train to get over the top and down the other side. Nevertheless, by unhitching the horses and with the help of many helping hands, the stagecoach did get turned around and on its way back.

By early evening, oxen puffing and steaming, the first section of the wagon train, the Italians, topped the grade and by nightfall reached the city. The others came in close behind.

The word "City" should never have been applied to what appeared to be nothing more than a relay station for whomever. A couple of flat top, dirt floor, stone walled structures with most of their windows shot out, and a rickety shack for a saloon was about all there was to this so-called city. There was, however, plenty of open space for the wagon train to circle around and make camp. The handful of people who lived there were obviously delighted to have company, but as for food and lodging for the stagecoach passengers, if they didn't mind whisky for dinner and sleeping on the dirt floor, one could say it was quite accommodating since that's about all that was there.

With darkness closing in there was no way the stagecoach

Dago Red! Westward - Ho!

could be expected to continue its journey, especially since by the time campfires were crackling, fry pans and skillets sizzling and, for the Italians, pots boiling ready to toss in the pasta, the coach driver and his side kick riding shotgun were drunker than mourners at an Irish Wake.

Realizing the plight of the hungry passengers who for the most part hadn't spoken to each other since the earlier confrontation, the Italians, hats in hand, approached them with an offer they couldn't refuse: join them for an Italian-style (God only knows what went into the sauce) pasta and sourdough bread dinner with an abundance of wine to wash it down. Considering the location and conditions, a banquet, no less. Needless to say, no one refused the offer.

Having been on a steady diet of grits and (bacon grease) fried squirrel innards, Reverend Gadwall could not resist the tempting aroma of Italian cooking wafting his way. Hat in hand he cautiously approached the scene of the banquet. The need to ask if he may join the feeding frenzy was negated by the slapping of a plate of cheese-crowned pasta and chunk of crispy sourdough bread in his free hand, followed by the dropping of his hat in order to clutch the overflowing goblet of wine being thrust in the other. Speechless, he glanced at the offerings, then to the host who quickly set about serving others. The least he could do now was to utter grace:

"Thank you Oh Lord, for creating such fine people. Amen!"

He was quite impressed with how well the food related to the wine, and vice versa. This was, in fact, his very first time with the wine experience, and in low audible tones he so stated:

"These Catholics have something here," he mumbled.

"And their priests, God's advocates, they've got it made ... hmm, I wonder? I'm God's advocate as well, am I not . . .?"

Without giving it a second thought, he headed for the

wine wagon where the wine was being dispensed directly from the barrel, repeatedly stepping in line for a refill.

As is the custom with Italians, after dinner the reveling commenced, dancing to the music that resounded throughout the high crags well into the night. However, Reverend Gadwall, not being much for dancing, chose to remain at the wine barrel, hovering constantly around the spigot like a wine gnat during barrel tasting.

As old Giuseppe stomped around swinging his wife Maria in a skirt-flaring, whirling tango step, she kept glancing in the direction of her daughter and John at the edge of the campfires' glow, framed against the rising full moon, holding hands, pulling their bodies ever closer to each other, a disturbing sight to Maria.

"Giuseppe," she said, "you better have a talk with your daughter before . . . well, you know . . . in case you haven't noticed."

"Ah yes," he answered. "I noticed the two young ones eyeing each other, and now . . . well . . . yes, I will talk to them. Besides, my old legs are about to give out on me anyway."

As her father approached, Giuseppina took a step back while loosening her grip on John's hands.

"Papa, please," she said with a slight tremor to her voice.

"I know what you're thinking, but we are just trying to be friends . . . nothing more."

"Nothing more?" questioned her father. "You sure?"

"Well . . . yes, Papa."

"And you, young man. Your name is John? Mister Jeb's son?" he asked, knowing quite well who he was.

"Yes sir, I'm John, but please, listen . . ."

"And your only interest in my daughter is just as a . . . friend?"

"Sir, if I was to say that, I'd be lying, and that I will not do."

"Now, that's much better! And you, Giuseppina, your mother and I would hope that we raised a wholesome, healthy, normal young woman. Would you care to add something

Dago Red! Westward - Ho!

... maybe like your true feelings ... in your heart ... No?"

"Yes, Papa, I would," she answered. Firming up her emotions, she stammered: "I ... I ... well, I ... I, Papa, please," she pleaded.

"Giuseppina, the word is "love," is it not? With a young man like this, and such a balmy moonlit night, if there were not a spark of love in your heart, surely I'd think you were sick. And as for you, young man, having lived for nearly a century I do consider myself well qualified to judge your integrity. So, give me your word that you will not disgrace or compromise my daughter's reputation."

"Sir, I love your daughter. I would hope that someday, when settled and proved worthy, you would grant me your daughter's hand in marriage. In the meantime, regardless of my feelings, I'd never let matters go so far as to disgrace or, as you put it, compromise, Giuseppina. She means much more to me than that."

Impressed, cracking a comforting smile, Giuseppe, while putting his arm around his daughter, addressed the two young lovers:

"Enough has been said. You have my blessing. Go! The moon is beckoning, take advantage of it, but control your emotions lest ... well, as it sometimes happens ... well, I'm sure you know what I mean." The final instruction was:

"John, when the dancing and music stops, be sure that Giuseppina is back here. No later!"

"Well, what did you accomplish? I do not see our daughter at your side," questioned Maria of her husband.

"I assure you, Maria, Giuseppina will be all right. John is a fine, sensible young man. We need not worry," he assured.

"On a night like this? Be all right? At her age? Giuseppe, have you lost your senses?"

"No, I have not lost my senses and neither will our daughter lose her virginity, that I assure you."

"You ... of all people, truly believe that? Have you

forgotten what happened with us?"

"I haven't forgotten, and I haven't forgotten that you were a year younger than your daughter at the time, and that it was you, not I, who was the aggressor . . . or have you forgotten that?"

The comment not only hit a nerve with Maria, but also drew a sharp reprimand: "Shut up! Say not another word, you old fool!"

"All right, all right, so I'm an old fool. Do you want to dance with me, or . . .?" he responded with a sparkle in his eye and a flick of his eyebrows.

"First we'll dance, then we'll . . . my God . . . you old billy goat . . . you!" exclaimed Maria, likewise with a devilish sparkle in her eye.

Come morning, the pleasing aroma of fresh brewed coffee overpowering the smell of crackling sagebrush campfires aroused the stagecoach travelers from a restless sleep. Not even the wine they'd consumed the night before could compensate for the hardness of the ground they'd slept on. But, some coffee brewed cowboy style sure as heck would help.

Breakfast being a big thing with the pioneers, as was dinner with the Italians, the pioneers extended breakfast invitations for coffee, bacon and biscuits to the travelers. The offer was accepted graciously, not hesitating to step up once the ladle rattling against a pot announced:

"Come and get it!"

Their differences now forgotten, the travelers and stagecoach driver chatted as they sipped hot coffee from tin cans. The rising sun casting its rays on the distant plateau was a sight to behold. But even more so were the sun-highlighted puffs of smoke drifting skyward in the clear still morning air from distant high points. The Italians, having witnessed this phenomenon at their last stopover, still unsure what it all meant, announced excitedly:

Dago Red! Westward - Ho!

"Look, there it is again! What does it mean?"

Camp chores and activities ceased as they gathered in groups wondering what the Indians were talking about at such an early hour. It soon became obvious, considering the size of the caravan of prairie schooners, the encounter with the band of Indians at the North Platte River and the cavalry's presence at the time, that they, the caravan, in the opinion of the pioneers, were the topic of discussion. To a point they were right, but it was only the Italian contingency that was being discussed and not the pioneers per se.

Attention shifted to the coach driver as he commented about the ongoing smoke signaling in the distance. He'd been out West for more years then he ever thought he would or really cared to be. Although he could not interpret the signal code word for word, he did know enough from past experience that these particular smoke signals meant trouble for someone. Many times his stagecoach had been chased all over Hell's Creation right after one of these transcontinental forays of communication between Indians.

What he didn't know was that it was the substance contained in the report from the two sneaky Indians (Chief Many Horse's scouts) who were spying on the Italians the day before when the double barrel shotgun discharged setting off what appeared to them as a cannonade. And as is the custom with government reports, they garnished and twisted it to the extent that it portrayed the bell as the most awesome secret weapon ever devised by man. And that had it not been for their extensive training, elite in their field of gathering military intelligence, and based on what they'd experienced with the weapon, which they exaggerated to no end, half the Indian Nation could very well be wiped out from just one volley of multiple cannon balls discharged from this awesome secret weapon in the hands of these mysterious new-comers to their lands.

But Chief No Horse was not going along with this, considering how they'd been rescued and befriended, and who were now referring to the Italians as "The Mighty Messiahs" and not a threat to their kind.

Gathered around the coach driver, his passengers especially worried, they and the pioneers watched with interest and wonder at this spectacular display of wireless, visual, silent and instant, but effective, conversation going on between the two tribes miles and miles apart. The Italians, less concerned, also took note but nevertheless went about their chores in preparation of moving on. The coach driver could only make out a little of the highly technical part of the back and forth series of smoke signals between Chief Many Horse and his cousin Chief No Horse. However, the common language he did understand and therefore interpreted accordingly:

"Cousin Chief No Horse, are you back on line?"

"Yes," came the answer with an added comment:

"But I don't go along with you!"

"All right, we'll get the other tribes on line too. They best get in on this!"

Within minutes smoke signals drifted skyward from all directions as the "get on line" message was relayed from one tribe to the next. Once all were on line, the smoky haze from their signal fires drifted for miles. With formalities now behind them, the two cousins continued while the others eagerly listened in.

"My scouts were attacked by your so-called friends!" read the series of smoke puffs from Chief Many Horse's signal fires.

"They were besieged by a cannonade of horrendous proportions discharged from the secret weapon you made reference to! These people, whoever they are, pose a serious threat!"

Dago Red! Westward - Ho!

"It cannot be! You've got to be mistaken!" came the concerned answer. "And what about the vino?"

"Mistaken my foot. You yourself said that they possessed such a weapon, and that they were aggressive fighters! Did you not? And this vino thing, have you been chewing loco weed?" The question mark appeared well pronounced in the distance.

"But wait a minute! Hold your damned horses! Your jumping to conclusions!" responded Chief No Horse, then continued:

"Your scouts saw the barrel wagon, did they not?"

"They did. So what?"

"If it were not such a precious cargo, would they be protecting it with a cannon?"

"You know Cousin No Horse, I think you got something there."

The ensuing argument between the two chiefs coupled with the added comments of the other tribes grew to such proportions that the smoke from their signal fires had fouled the sky to the extent that the coach driver could no longer make out the messages being relayed. For that matter, the messages got so garbled that neither could the Indians. Pressed for answers, the coach driver stated bluntly:

"I can tell you this: someone, somehow, has stirred up trouble! They make reference to a huge cannon, a volley of cannon fire back there somewhere. Although there seems to be some disagreement. The signals coming from further east appear to be friendly. Some mention of a pleasureful beverage, color of ox blood. Can't make out what they call it though."

"That certainly leaves us out. We have no cannon. And for that matter, aside from that little friendly tribe befriended by the Italians here, we haven't as much as even seen an Indian, let alone engaged him in battle. I don't believe we need have any concern," assured Elder Jeb.

Although reassuring, the coach driver still had his concerns:

"It's no problem with you folks since you are now heading Southwest towards Fort Bridger. But we're heading Northeast. We're liable to head into a war party before we reach Fort Laramie and head due East again."

"I see your point . . . well . . . we can spare a day or two. What say we all stay put and see what develops?" volunteered Elder Jeb.

Giving thought to the risks involved versus the good time they had the night before, the stagecoach passengers persuaded their driver to take up the offer. It was resolved. They'd stay over. "We'll not trust to luck," stated the driver. Reverend Gadwall, still reeling from the drinking bout of the night before, was quick to seize the moment:

"Gentlemen, you need not trust to luck; put your trust in the Good Lord and you will . . ." Before the sentence could be finished, the man riding shotgun interrupted by stating:

"If you don't mind, reverend, when I'm dead I'll put my soul in the trust of the Good Lord all right, but as long as I'm alive, I'll put my trust in 'Old Betsy' here," he said while slapping the stock of the double barrel, rabbit eared shotgun he was cradling.

Realizing the futility of trying to preach Christianity to these western roughnecks, the reverend shuffled over to the Italians who were busying themselves with the chore of pulling up stakes.

"You folks pulling out . . . on your own?" asked the Reverend somewhat worried.

"Yes," responded Capo Giuseppe. "We best move on. We are slow, you will catch up."

"Oh my God!" thought the reverend. "The wine? What about the wine?" The thought of losing the wine to the Indians crashed through his mind with the full force of prayer.

"No, you must not go!" he pleaded. "Think of your wi...

I mean, wives and . . . and the children!" Obviously he had wine on his mind but caught himself in time.

"Oh . . . but we do not worry, Mister Reverend. We have faith in God, he will look after us. I'm sure you understand, do you not?"

"Yes . . . yes, I understand. Trust in God, but . . . but the wine, maybe God . . . you know . . . wine and there's the Indians. Maybe you should remain here with us so we can help you drin . . . I mean, guard your wi . . . I mean . . . your wives," stammered Reverend Gadwall in confusion. He was desperate. Now that he'd partaken of the pleasures of drinking wine, the thought of losing it was the utmost thing on his mind. Nor was he too sure he'd want to trust all that wine in the hands of the Good Lord alone.

"Indians? We have met them, they are good people. We do not mind sharing our wine with them."

"Lord have mercy! No! Not that! Share the wine with Indians? Good God!" the thought of it caused the Reverend to panic. Falling a shade short of running, he sashayed over to the pioneer camp just as fast as his chubby legs would shuffle. Puffing hard, he blurted out the problem at hand:

"The Italians . . . the wine . . . their wives . . . Indians. Oh my God! We have to do something!"

"Reverend, for the love of . . . Christ! Slow down. Get hold of yourself," pleaded Elder Jeb. "Now take a deep breath, hold it a minute, then exhale and start all over again," he suggested.

Eager to get the message across right, the Reverend did just that. He sucked enough air into his massive lung cavity to nearly launch himself aloft to the tree tops. To Jeb standing toe to toe with the Reverend and the few people who had moved in close to hear him out, the inhalation procedure was not bothersome. But when he finally exhaled, the syphoning of wine-saturated gut gasses from his stomach was as putrid as the discharge from a brandy still. Backing off and gasping, as did the others, Elder Jeb remarked:

"My God . . . reverend . . . ! How much wine . . . did you drink last night?"

"Oh . . . the wine, yes, but you see . . . their wives, I mean...and, and . . ."

Cutting the reverend's stammering short, Jeb felt obligated to pass on what he knew about the Italians, especially the Sicilians, regarding their women.

"Reverend!" said Jeb firmly, "If you at all value your reproductive organs, I suggest you back off on this wife thing lest you get them sliced off and rammed down your throat! Those people may be generous with their wine, but not their women! Surely you recall what happened to Mister Harvey?"

"No . . . no! You misunderstand, Jeb. It's not the women, it's the wine! The Indians will get it for sure unless . . . unless . . . don't you see?" In all his stammering it did trigger a sudden thought:

"That little band of Indians? Drinking wine? The huge bell? The shotgun blasts? The smoke signals? Of course, that's it!"

Leaving the reverend standing there without explanation, Elder Jeb strode over to the coach driver and excitedly stated:

"Our fears are unfounded. Here, take a look," he said, calling attention to the bell wagon. "What does that look like to you?"

"Why, a cannon of sorts. That never occurred to me. But the volley . . . ? The cannonade . . . ? How do you explain that?"

"Remember the shotgun discharge at the pass? The echo ricocheting down the canyon? They'd been following us and thought they'd been fired upon . . . don't you think?"

"You know, you could be right!"

"Of course I'm right. And that friendly little band of Indians, they'd drunk the wine, more than enough to appreciate it, and therefore are refusing to take an aggressive stand against . . . at least the Italians. And it's only the

Italians that the issue is all about."

"I agree," said the coach driver, "I'll explain it to my passengers. We're pulling out!"

No sooner had the discussion ended than the same Regiment of Cavalry came into view heading back to Fort Laramie at a fast pace. With a wave of hand from the Colonel, they pulled up short amidst a cloud of dust. Following a graceful dismount, the Colonel, slapping the dust off his uniform, walked up to the men and said:

"You folks all right up here?" Although obvious, he chose to ask the question anyway.

"Those smoke signals had us worried." By now the smoke haze had drifted Eastward, leaving only minute traces to mark their locations.

"They had us worried also, but we now feel that there is no real threat," responded Elder Jeb.

"I'm glad to hear that. We were quite surprised when we saw it. Actually, we've had very little trouble with the Indians up here, at least not lately. That is with the exception of that weird bunch further West headed up by old Chief Crooked Finger."

"That's a relief. We're also heading back up to Fort Laramie, then East. Mind if a couple of your men ride tail for us? My passengers are a little edgy," stated the coach driver.

"I can't blame them none. Yes, we can do that, but the real threat is not with the Indians," offered the Colonel. Then addressing the others as well, he proceeded to explain their true purpose for being in the field:

"There's been an atrocious massacre down at Mountain Meadows south of Salt Lake City. A whole train of emigrants, aside from the children who were kidnaped and taken, all the men and women, some one hundred or so, were literally butchered, knifed, shot and killed."

"My God! Who'd do a thing like that? And why?" asked

Elder Jeb as the others listened in eagerly.

"The finger points to Brigham Young's religious fanatics, and only because the emigrants gave shelter to a handful of their defectors and they were killed as well."

"Good gracious, have they been taken into custody?"

"Not yet. We know they did it, but they have friends in high places, if you know what I mean."

Without going into further detail, the Colonel then advised them:

"Be aware at all times. Do not give sanctuary to any known Bigamists. They may be defectors. The perpetrators may be disguised and pose as Indians. Keep your guns at the ready regardless of how you are approached, and that includes when approached with a white flag displayed, that's what caught the emigrants off guard."

Shifting his attention to the wine wagon, the Colonel asked:

"Are those wine barrels . . . ? Filled with wine . . . ?"

Apparently due to the circumstances at the time, he hadn't noticed the wagon on their previous encounter.

Nodding toward Giuseppe, Elder Jeb commented:

"I believe this old gentleman could best answer that . . . Sir."

Capo Giuseppe, removed his hat as he stepped forward.

"Yes, Colonel . . . wine," he answered to both questions.

"You see, it is our custom . . ."

"Yes, of course. I forgot. You folks are Italians. Well, I must warn everyone. Brigham Young's crowd follows the Mormon Faith to the letter, and alcohol is a devil's brew as far as they're concerned. If detected, they will take the wine away from you, destroy it, and possibly harm you as well."

"Destroy our wine? No! That will never come to pass! Wine is our life!" stated Giuseppe, somewhat shaken.

"I understand, but it could cost you . . . your life!"

"My life is no longer of much importance," responded Giuseppe with the meaningful expression of an old man who has seen it all and, aside from the well being of his family, cares less for his own life.

The mention of wine brought Reverend Gadwall up closer to the conversing pair. The thought of the wine being lost to his despised religious counterparts, the Mormons, raised the hackles on the back of his neck. Like a fighting rooster positioning himself to pounce on his opponent, he shuffled up closer as if to take on all comers.

"If the Italians lose the wine, then so will I. Totally unthinkable," he thought. Being a man of the cloth, although of different cloth texture, the Mormons who worshiped a non-wine drinking Bigamist God, assumed not to savor or recognize wine as the blood of Christ as the Catholics believed, and which he now believed to be true also, the reverend regardless of what religious faith be his plighted troth, if the Mormons were to sample the wine, they too may become believers in wine, the Catholic way, and as sure as he was as round as he was tall, hijack the entire load of wine thus leaving nary a drop for him or, for that matter, the Italians. On the other hand, if they chose not to sample the wine and therefore do in fact destroy it, the disastrous end result would be the same.

Akin to the splattering, crushing effect of the pumpkin to the head that unseated Ichabod Crane from his horse, catapulted from the hands of his tormenter, the Headless Horseman, the impact of the exploding unthinkable thought sent the reverend reeling backwards, stumbling and falling to the ground in a dust-generating roll accompanied by the wailing sounds of a bull elk in rut.

Accustomed to their jackasses' habits of performing similar rituals, rolling and braying after a hard day on the trail, Jake, the mule skinner, not knowing what had transpired, nevertheless being the best qualified to deal with the situation, came running to the reverend's aid who, in his frenzied attempts to regain control had wedged himself between a log and a rock. Having experienced their mules caught up in similar situations, no less than four men to the team, each with a firm hold on the reverends limbs, the mule skinners uprighted him. Inquisitively, Jake then asked:

"Reverend, what the devil happened?"

The reverend, still shattered by the revolation of this devastating thought, replied:

"Yes . . . yes, that's it! They're Devils! The wine! Yes, the wine! Oh Heaven forbid, don't let those Devils get the wine!"

"Reverend, for God's sake, calm down," insisted Jake as Giuseppe, scratching his chin, looked on.

"And their God . . . oh my! And all his wives . . . they'll drink it all for sure! Stop them! Stop them!" he blurted.

"Mister Jake," said Giuseppe in a somewhat thoughtful manner, "bring him over to our camp. My people know what to do," he stated in an reassuring manner. Retrieving the Reverend's hat, beating the dust off of it and jamming it on his head, Jake did just that.

By the time he'd downed the second goblet of wine, Reverend Gadwall was back to his senses. But, the thought of losing the wine still weighed heavily on his mind, as it did with Giuseppe.

The stress of their ordeal, trudging across country with one crisis after another continually cropping up was beginning to take its toll on Giuseppe. Aside from his immediate family, even if they knew for sure, no one was aware that within a few days, on his next birthday, he'd reach the century mark: One Hundred Years Old. But regardless of his age, he was determined to see it through. Firmly he stated:

"We will not take the risk of losing the wine! There must be another way!"

The Italians could not afford to lose the wine, but neither

could the Reverend, or at least he didn't care to. Reverend Gadwall might have been short on logic, but certainly not on brains. Having noticed that there was no priest amongst the Italians and being aware of their strong religious ties with God, be he a devoted wine drinker or not, and figuring that there's soon to be a parting of the ways, he'd best throw his lot in with the Italians. And so, hat in hand, he propositioned the Italians. Addressing Capo Giuseppe directly he offered:

"You folks have been so kind that I feel obligated to offer you my services as God's Advocate, at least until such time as you have built your Church of Worship and are therefore assigned a Frocked Clergyman."

The words used being somewhat unfamiliar to old Giuseppe, he questioned:

"You mean . . . like a Priest? Be our Priest? Say Mass?"

"Well . . . yes, you could say that."

A short discussion amongst the Italian Elders, and the Reverend was in. They'd concluded that they were in fact being conned, but then, what the heck, they had plenty of wine and, of course, no priest.

Giving serious thought to their predicament, Giuseppe approached the Colonel with a question and accompanied explanation:

"Is there any other route we can take? You see, we have little in the way of armament, and even if we did, we'd have no desire to use it. And we certainly do not want to lose the wine."

Before the colonel could answer, several of the pioneers, mule skinners included, proposed that they stay with the caravan regardless, under their protection.

"Does that answer your question?" asked the Colonel.

"No . . . Sir. We shall not permit ourselves to become a burden to our friends here!"

"Well then, it's somewhat slower, but you can take the Northerly route. When you get to Green River, head upstream a ways, then over the pass heading due West again and you will sooner or later come across the Oregon Trail somewhere along the line. You'll know it when you see it, what with all the broken down wagons and discarded furniture strewn along the way. Eventually you'll come to where the trail branches off. The left arm will lead you South and eventually take you into Northern California, and the right arm will lead you North to Southern Oregon. They're both rough going," he said with an added warning.

"Keep in mind what I said about what happened down at Mountain Meadows, what may appear to be friendly Indians could be Mormons with ill intent. And, keep an eye out for old Chief Crooked Finger."

Applying the wisdom gained over the span of a century, old Giuseppe responded:

"Thank you Colonel. We will take our chances. That is the route we will take."

Reverend Gadwall grinned sheepishly; he'd guessed it right. Unraveling an old double barreled flint lock from it's deerskin wrappings, he proudly displayed the weapon as he assuredly announced:

"Leave the matter of the wine to me, I assure you whether they be Mormans or Indians, under my protection, the wine is secure."

CHAPTER 9

Having reached Green River, the Italians bid farewell to the pioneers. It was a solemn parting to say the least. The last that could be seen of the Italian caravan was Reverend Gadwall's overburdened pony close on the heels of the wine wagon, with the Reverend sitting in the saddle, sucking in the wafting wine fumes, his old long rifle perched over his shoulder like a garden rake.

John seated on his horse, hat in hand with fixed stare towards the parting wagons that were carrying away his beloved Giuseppina, with an ache in his heart and a prayer on his lips, sadly stated:

"May God care for you, My Love."

A short distance away his father, Jeb, commented to his son's mother:

"Martha," he said sympathetically, "do you see what I see?"

"Yes, Jeb," she replied, "like father, like son. And I can't say that I blame him none. She's a beautiful girl."

It wasn't the well pronounced trail that they'd been on previously, but certainly passable. Each day when looking to the North, they could see smoke signals in the distance spiraling upwards. It was obvious, the dispute between Chief No Horse and his cousin Chief Many Horse had now extended to the other tribes, each taking sides for their own reasons. There were those who believed that Chief No Horse had indeed come across the nectar of life, the beverage he referred to as "Vino." But what could they do about it? By now the Italian caravan had moved out of their jurisdiction, working its way into the jurisdiction of a radical, weird tribe made up of outcast members from various Indian Tribes who would have nothing to do with them. The weirdest of them all, a screwball at best, being none other than the Chief himself, Chief Crooked Finger.

Convinced that maybe there was something to this "vino" thing and that maybe he had indeed missed out on a good thing, Chief Many Horse decided to call upon his Ute buddy, Chief Heap Big Salt (so named because he'd cornered the salt market, and understandably so since the Great Salt Lake was his territory and therefore supplied the Mormons with salt as well as the many Indian tribes), figuring that the Italians were now skirting the edge of his domain and that he might therefore agree to dispatch a contingency of braves to intercept the caravan before Chief Crooked Finger and his gang of nitwits could get to them. No telling what they'd do once hooked on the "vino." They were crazy enough without that. They were so far off the wall that most of their neighboring tribes had, in some manner or another and for whatever reason, had a run in with them.

The Nez Perce Tribe to the North swore that if they ever again wandered into their area of influence, they'd get a hell of a lot more than their noses pierced.

They'd screwed the Shoshone Tribe out of shoes and moccasins as well as other garments and trinkets and were therefore booted out of their territory.

The Cheyenne and Arapaho had a bounty on them of two buffalo hides for each one of his warriors brought in, dead or alive, and a virgin squaw thrown in for bringing in Chief Crooked Finger himself.

The Ute Indian chief, Heap Big Salt, having been paid with counterfeit wampum for a load of salt, had a judgement for same against what he referred to as those "crooked, cockeyed, counterfeiting creeps."

Dago Red! Westward - Ho!

Since they were not recognized as a bonafide Chartered Tribe by the Indian Nations, affairs of state via smoke signal would never be relayed to them, so being isolated such as they were, they never knew what was going on, and cared less.

Having made their first encampment on fairly high ground, again as the sun was setting in the West, the Italians stood in awe at the sight of smoke signals spiraling upward, high in the distance, North of where they'd come. It was Chief Many Horse transmitting long distance to his Ute buddy, asking him to get on line. Knowing that there would be a response, the Italians trained their eyes until, sure enough, they sighted an equally high rising spiral of smoke made up of dots and dashes, however not from the West, East or North as before, but from due South from the direction of the Great Salt Lake. Chief Heap Big Salt had, in spite of the distance, received the message and was acknowledging same by asking a dual question:

"What's up buddy? Need salt?"

"No! Something much better!"

"What's better than salt?"

"Vino! The nectar of life, the stimulant of sex! So says my Cousin," answered Chief Many Horse.

"Vino?" questioned his Ute buddy. "Stimulant of . . . sex? Never heard of it! I deal in salt, saltpeter to suppress sex, lest the country be overrun with Bring-em-Young's crowd, what with all them wives!"

Well, the Italians knew that something big was in the wind, but obviously didn't know what, only that the Indians were no doubt referring to them, of which the subsequent discussion definitely was. The correspondence continued:

"All right, so you don't want salt. And I don't deal in this . . . vino . . . stuff. So how can I help you?" asked Chief Heap Big Salt in a series of smoke bursts.

"I want you to do me a favor, if you can," read the

return answer followed by a long oratory explaining the need and purpose for intercepting the Italian caravan.

"Sorry, can't help you. My braves are all committed. We have our hands full, what with those mad men out at Salt Lake City. You know, Bring-em-Young and his crowd of bigamists going around killing any man that doesn't have a dozen or so wives."

"The hell you say?" questioned Chief Many Horse. "A dozen or so wives? They must be well balled and drinking a lot of . . . vino!"

"Balled, yes, vino, no, salt, yes. Not just plain salt, I've been selling them 'saltpeter.' Gotta get them horney buggers under control, you know."

"Well that accounts for their killing spree. They've got the wherewithal and the wives but can't perform. No wonder the poor buggers are going mad! You devil, you!"

"Yep! And that's what you call 'Hell,' Old Buddy!"

Continuing on their journey the Italians finally came to the point where the road split. The Southerly route was ruled out because it appeared to be leading them into dusty, desolate, desert country. But then so was the Northerly route ruled out what with its menacing, snow-capped, jagged peaks looming up in the distance, whereas straight ahead, although a poorly marked trail and seldom used, looked perfectly fine and the way to go. So they took it.

What they didn't know was, why was it seldom used? The reason being that it led right smack into the middle of Chief Crooked Finger's Domain. Unaware of the perils that lie ahead, they rumbled along to where by mid-afternoon they arrived in the middle of a patch of sagebrush, cradled in the bosom of high plateaus on either side. Maneuvering their wagons accordingly, they made camp. They couldn't have picked a nuttier place to settle down had they chosen to camp on the front lawn of an Insane Asylum.

Dago Red! Westward - Ho!

Since the day they had parted company with the pioneers, Giuseppina kept up her vigil, always with the vision of seeing her lover John, astride his galloping steed, rushing to her yearning, loving arms.

At times, a spiral of wind whipped dust appearing in the distance from whence they'd come, brought about a gasp of excitement, but then as it faded, a feeling of despair. Here again, as others busied themselves with the camp chores, she stood on high ground, the high desert wind to her back, framing her flowered dress against her Goddess-like figure, her wavy jet black hair responding to the will of the wind. It, too, as her garment, appearing to want to hustle her back into John's arms. Her plight was so obvious that every member of the caravan seemed to suffer along with her, especially her parents. Joining her daughter, Maria, without questioning her feelings, offered a measure of condolence:

"Giuseppina," she said, "we understand the feelings within you, but you cannot carry on like this."

"Mother," she responded, "if I thought I'd never see him again, I would die." As the statement was made she buried her tear-dampened face in her mother's arms and sobbed:

"I hope he's all right."

"Cry, go ahead and cry. It is natural for a person with love and compassion in their heart to cry. But listen carefully to me," she added. "If he truly loves you, and I'm sure that he does, he will come to you. That I promise. The flame of love is not so easily extinguished. Believe me, I know. Come now, let's go to your father. I don't think he's feeling very well."

Little did either one know that John, with his father's blessing, was riding hard to catch up to them. With a minimum of provisions and a Winchester Rifle jammed into its saddle scabbard, from daybreak to sunset, he followed the deep ruts left by the wine wagon that neither wind nor rain in all its fury could erase.

During the evening meal Maria noticed her husband fidgeting with his food. Aside from an occasional sip of wine, he took little nourishment. Before she could comment, Giuseppe rose to his feet, wandered to the outer edge of the campfire's glow, wine goblet in hand, gazed towards the East admiring the rising moon. She joined him, taking in the sounds of the desert, coyotes howling and yipping in the distance, the shrill cry of the screech owls as they skimmed over the sagebrush, its fragrant blooms glistening in the moonlight. Grasping his free hand and holding it firmly she expressed concern:

"Giuseppe," she said, "you are not yourself tonight. What is it, are you not feeling well?"

"Do you know what day this is?" he asked.

"Yes, I know," she replied while turning her head towards him. "It is your birthday."

"Well, I feel that this one is my last," he said with a quiver in his voice. She gasped, trembled but remained silent as he continued.

"And maybe rightfully so. One Hundred years is a long time to have lived. This is not what you'd like to hear me say, but I will not make it through the night," he said solemnly.

"But I die content. I've had a good life, and where on earth is there a better place or time to die but in a land of freedom and beauty. Maria, listen to those sounds, look at that moon! How many times have we sipped wine and made love in the light of the moon? And what pleases me most of all, Giuseppina has found love."

Sobbing softly, her response was tears glistening in the moonlight as they rolled down across the smile on her face, for regardless of the sorrow in her heart, her reassuring comfort was ever present. That was the last thing he saw or heard, as the goblet slipped from his hand then slumped to the ground.

Next morning at the crack of dawn, while the women folks and the kids busied themselves with the camp chores, several men dug old Giuseppe's grave while others prepared a coffin befitting a Capo. The reverend, saddened by the loss of his newly made friend, shuffled the pages of his little black Bible in search of the best sermon he could possibly find within its weathered pages. Since they'd left Saint Joseph, he'd been hoping for just such an occasion where he could put his talents to use. But now that the time had come, he was at a loss for words. He was deeply impressed in the manner the grave site was dug, the coffin was made, and above all, the elaborate configuration and placing of the needed apparatus to dispense and receive the ingredients that would insure eternal life and sustain his soul on the long but glorious journey to the Promised Land.

Having placed the deceased in the coffin and all else in place, Reverend Gadwall embarked on a long, tedious oratory as the uncontaminated, pure desert soil was being shoveled back into the grave. He continued on until high noon, at which time he joined the others in raising their wine-filled goblets in a final "Salute!" to their departed Capo. Surely St. Peter got the message and was therefore oiling the rusty hinges of the Pearly Gates of Heaven in preparation of receiving, although rare, the soul of a deserving mortal human being.

All being in readiness, the caravan pulled out, rumbling across the rough terrain, sending out seismic vibrations through Earth's subterranean stratus that extended under and beyond the surrounding plateaus.

CHAPTER 10

Old Chief Crooked finger (so named because of the long standing Indian tradition of a child being named according to what it's father first sees at the instant he steps out of his wigwam to first announce its birth or an unusual event that takes place, or something unusual about the child, in this case a paralyzed crooked index finger), was aroused from his midday nap by the strange and unfamiliar seismic earth vibrations originating somewhere in the distance. Rising to his feet, he draped his skinny, bone-protruding, sun-baked body with a buffalo hide, adorned his head with his high ranking, eagle-feathered head piece, picked up his multi-painted war staff and authoritatively marched out of his wigwam and into the center of the compound. He'd correctly concluded that someone had wandered into his domain, but who? And with what? Right arm outstretched with its gnarled and sinewy muscles glistening in the midday sun, paralyzed crooked index finger pointing at a ninety degree angle from its intended direction, he commanded:

"Fetch Left Ear! Bring him to me at once!"

With that short, to the point command, a runner was dispatched to summon the official tracker, Left Ear (so named for his abnormally shaped ear, in this case much like a toilet plunger).

However, the tracker needn't be summoned because he was already aroused from his midday nap by the same mysterious vibrations, and just stepping out of his wigwam intent on reporting to the Chief when the runner rushed up and yelled out the command at the top of his voice, directly into the tracker's left ear:

"Left Ear! Come quick! The Chief . . ." The announcement, however, was cut short by the tracker's hand being clamped across the mouth of the runner, followed by a cursing, dressing down:

"You dumb son-of-a-cockroach! You know better than to yell in my left ear . . . damn it!" he swore. As sensitive as his hearing was, due to the abnormality of the instrument receiving the sound waves and then gathering them up in concentrated form, then ramming it all into the inner ear, with the equally abnormal tuning forks sending the now compounded sound waves screaming through channels directly into the brain, thus causing a possible meltdown of same, the dressing down was surely justified.

Upon approaching the Chief, the tracker, with the runner close at his heels, gave the sign of acknowledgment of the Chief's authority by first glancing towards the distant mountain where dwelled the Spirits of their forefathers, their Gods as they believed them to be, then back to the Chief. Following the protocol of custom, the Chief spoke first. Taking it for granted, he said:

"You have apparently sensed the mysterious rumblings and vibrations. What do you make of it? What is it? Who is it?"

Having yet to fully recover from the near brain meltdown, the tracker answered:

"Not buffalo, not cattle herd, not horses."

Giving thought to the answer, the Chief fired another question:

"I didn't ask you what it wasn't. I asked you . . . what is it?"

The tracker trying to get his brain back into gear answered:

"Not Cavalry, not wagon train, not thunder."

"Damn it!" screamed the Chief. "Tell me what it is! Not what it isn't! And who it is! Not who it isn't! What the hell's the matter with you? Is your brain locked up?"

The commotion had now attracted the rest of the

braves. They gathered around their Chief and the tracker in a tight circle with the war council members crowding to the front, thus forcing the runner in between the Chief and the tracker. With the war council's participation, they would now carry out the matter of the strange mysterious goings on somewhere in the distance. The arm waving and chattering escalated to the point of complete chaos. Being caught between the two principal characters, the hand and arm gestures nearly slapped the runner to death. If it were not for the irritated squaw's intervention, the braves would have no doubt thrashed themselves to a pulp. Equally irritated by his own wife's intervention, the Chief addressed her bluntly:

"Damn it! Go back to wigwam!" he commanded, then added:

"What the hell do you know about such matters anyway?"

But his wife, determined to have the last word, in a calm but contemptuous manner answered his question by firmly, but simply, saying with an added gesture of her finger:

"Why the heck don't you get your finger out of your ass and just go out there and find out first hand what this is all about!"

With that final comment, she, along with the rest of the squaws, retreated back to their quarters in hopes he and his braves, to the last man, would do just that. They were exploiting the opportunity to get their husbands out of camp, off their backs, or stomachs, whichever, lest the camp would be overrun with kids. Besides the fact that the braves were prone to be lazy and quite untidy, they were a nuisance around the camp anyway. A good housecleaning was indeed in order.

Stunned with the simple solution, the braves fell silent. A last and final order by the Chief sent them scrambling to make preparation. They'd leave next morning at first light. They'd get out of camp pronto lest they'd find themselves battling on two fronts, their wives in camp and the intruders, whomever and wherever they may be.

Dago Red! Westward - Ho!

CHAPTER 11

Still smarting from the ass chewing he got from his wife the night before, Chief Crooked Finger paced back and forth from one campfire to the other while waiting out the dawn. Despite the fact that he'd been denied access to his own bed and therefore forced to sleep amongst the dogs on the hard ground outside his wigwam, the Chief was still in command, at least as it pertained to the planned investigative war campaign waiting to be launched. But the reported fact that his oldest son, Two Dog (so named because when he was born the first thing his father saw as he stepped out of his wigwam was two dogs having sex, and since their wording for the sex act as it applied to man or beast was: "Uk-Uk, oowee-oowee, Uk-Uk," accompanied with a grunt before and after, quite cumbersome and vulgar to say the least, the Chief knew damned well that his wife would kill him if in fact he followed the old Indian tradition to the letter in naming his son, Two Dogs (grunt) Uk-Uk, oowee-oowee, Uk-Uk (grunt), so having cut it short to Two Dog pleased her, but infuriated the Spirits (Gods of the Mountain) to the extent that they cast a curse upon the poor child, giving him a horrendous sex drive), was not among them, threw him into a fitful rage. The truth of the matter was, that all the time that he should have been at his father's side, he was in fact in the sack, locked in sexual embrace with his new bride, Two Dove (so named as was Two Dog, only this involved two doves having sex instead of dogs). This was not uncommon for him, considering that since he'd reached puberty the curse had him trying to screw just about anything that was hot and hollow. But nevertheless, the incident was dealt with harshly to say the least.

"I want Two Dog out here now! Drag him out by the balls if you have to, but get him out here, now! Damn it!" barked the Chief.

And so the order was carried out to the letter and fortunately for the recipient of this harsh treatment, since the Gods having tampered with his sex genes and thus tainting him with queer sexual traits, heterozygous confusion, heterosexual tendencies and in a pinch sodomy, but so far had not fully displayed those symptoms, because had he, in the mood his father and the braves were in at the moment, in an act of asexualization, he would have been hog tied to a horse and dragged through the sage brush for neither the Indians, nor the Spirits, their Gods, tolerated such nonsense, not even amongst the dogs.

Realizing that his father, the Chief, had just about had it with him, Two Dog, despite his preference to remain behind, scurried around getting his gear together and preparing his steed for the tedious journey that lay ahead. As did the others, he gleaned strips and pieces of meat off the roasted coyote carcass left over from the previous two days and stuffed it into his buffalo scrotum pouch along with roasted acorns. These rations along with certain insects picked up along the way would have to sustain him until his return back to the campsite.

The dozen or so dogs, knowing that this was more of a war excursion rather than a hunting expedition, chose to remain in camp, especially since the coyote carcass remained impaled on the spit yet to be discarded. Once discarded, if they are not there to claim it, scavenging coyotes would surely get it.

Dago Red! Westward - Ho!

At first light Chief Crooked Finger mounted his steed as did the others, including the Medicine Man (so destined for the profession from childhood due to his abnormally long right hand middle finger), whom they referred to as such due to respect and, of course, the fact that he dealt with the sciences relative to health. And, since they were on a war footing, which meant there could be casualties, a medic amongst them was imperative. The Chief gave the order to move out to what was destined to be, if not a military campaign, a highly scientific investigation of a mysterious phenomenon taking place somewhere on the plains of Territorial Western Wyoming. It was their sworn duty to gather information and if need be, depending on its significance, report their findings to other neighboring tribes of the area, whether they were on speaking terms or not. However, since it could be expected that this whole affair may be the doings of the White Man, they armed themselves to the teeth with spears, tomahawks, bows and arrows, to say nothing of knives, just in case the need should arise to extricate the perpetrators from their domain by force. One thing for sure, they could not depend on any help from their neighboring tribes because they'd just as soon see them get their ass kicked as not.

The patrol moved along cautiously, when possible following creek beds, dry and wet, on occasion dropping into ravines and depressions, thus keeping a low profile. Other than occasional necessary instructions, mostly by grunts and hand gestures passed back down the line, the only sound that could be heard was an occasional soft clatter of hoofs on rocks for the horses themselves realized the importance of stealth at a time like this.

They headed in a South-Easterly direction, more East than South, that would take them across a wide expanse of desert and over a long but narrow tabletop plateau that they must also cross, however at an angle since the plateau ran due East to West, more or less splitting the desert. It was tracker Left Ear's opinion that it was there, somewhere beyond that plateau, that the mysterious vibrations were being generated, and so it was there that they must ride to, regardless of the fact that it would take the better part of the day to get there.

By midday they had reached the base of the plateau where the only freshwater spring within a full day's ride from any direction existed. Here they would now dismount, water their horses as well as themselves, nourish themselves with the rations they carried in their buffalo scrotums and, of course, whatever edible creatures they'd find in this harsh land. As they napped and rested, a small band of buffalo grazed contentedly nearby, inching their way towards the spring. To say the least, the scene was tranquil. But suddenly, a brave who had been studying the movements of the buffalo herd while relieving himself some distance from the others, having observed some unusual activity amongst the buffalo, came trotting up to the Chief expressing concern.

"What is it?" asked the Chief.

"It's Two Dog," answered the brave.

At the mention of his son, the Chief looked around and, sure enough, his son was not amongst the others. Worrisome, he asked:

"Where's Two Dog?"

Without putting it in words but rather in hand gestures directed in the direction of the buffalo herd, obviously led the Chief to believe that his son was about to slay a buffalo; as a matter of fact, his first.

"Good, we need fresh meat in camp," said the Chief, expressing satisfaction. But such was not the case.

"No meat!" exclaimed the brave.

"What do you mean, no meat? Then what the hell is he

doing out there if it's not for meat?"

"Two Dog at it again!" responded the brave, short and blunt.

"At it again? What's it this time? No . . . it can't be!"

"Yes, him screw'um buffalo heifer," came the answer.

"Damn it! Boot him in the ass! Get him out of there! Drag him back by the balls!"

Not satisfied with just an order, he continued:

"Damn him! And damn the two friggin' dogs the day he was born!" blasted the Chief. Then swinging around abruptly with his gnarled right arm raised to eye level, waving frantically, trying to interpret the garbled command emitting from the brain as to whether it be the arm or the crooked index finger that should be pointing toward the mountain where dwelled the Spirits, the Chief let out his final blast:

"And damn you, up there on the mountain, you double-crossing sons-of-coyotes!"

If that last and final statement didn't move the Spirits, certainly nothing else ever would.

Well, orders are orders. With the whole of the war council in full agreement, they dispatched two of their toughest and meanest of braves to carry out the Chief's orders. They weren't gone but a few minutes when they came trotting back empty handed.

"Now what?" demanded the now somewhat calmer Chief. But before receiving a response, he fired another question:

""Did you boot him in the ass?"

"No need, Chief. Buffalo bull butt Two Dog in the ass, but good," came the answer.

"Serves him right. Too bad the bull didn't rip his damn balls off," growled the Chief.

"Bull do that too," assured the bearer of these glad tidings.

"What?! By the Great Spirits of the Mountain, get him

back here!" Obviously the Chief hadn't really meant what he'd said, but then he had, in fact, insulted his Gods, and so . . .?

"Can't, him run too fast."

"Run, where?"

"Back to camp."

At that instant, the sky darkened, bolts of lightening accompanied with ear-splitting thunder hit the ground at the heels of Two Dog, sending him running even faster in a zigzag pattern across the desert. Since sodomy had now become an issue, nothing less could be expected from their Gods, the Spirits of the Mountain. The Chief glanced towards the Medicine Man with raised eyebrows as if asking a question, but received nothing but a shrug of the shoulders, for there was nothing he could do about his son's behavior. Nevertheless, in a disgusting low ton and manner, not necessarily directed to the Medicine Man, the Chief uttered a final comment:

"I suppose it'll be a deer next."

Now, however, the Medicine Man was to respond while shaking his head in a "no-way" manner:

"No! Not possible!" he said firmly, then added:

"No can do. Deer run too fast."

Dago Red! Westward - Ho!

CHAPTER 12

The war council assured the Chief that this was in fact for the best. Let Two Dog go, he'd be nothing but a damned nuisance anyway. The Chief concurred. The platoon mounted up and moved on to carry out their intended mission, find the source of the mysterious vibration and rumbling sound waves that had surged through the earth's rock and sand for the better part of the afternoon of the previous day. Single file, they wound their way up the north slope of the plateau, across its tabletop, then to its southern perimeter where they now formed a line at its edge to scan the vastness of the desert below.

And as it was his duty to do so, Left Ear dismounted, pranced over to a large outcropping of solid rock, its base extending deep down past the base of the plateau, slapped his toilet plunger-like left ear up against its flat surface, vacuum suction forces holding his head firmly to the face of the rock much like an abalone found in submerged rocks of the Pacific Ocean, thus proceeded to register in his brain the various seismic vibrations and movements deep within the bowels of the earth, while his comrades scanned the earth's surface in order to detect the slightest of movements or sound and any unusual disturbances of the landscape. With this kind of a detection system in place, both above and below the crust of the earth, nothing, absolutely nothing of an unusual nature could possibly escape detection, a feat that could only be accomplished by a well-trained, properly equipped American Indian.

Like statues they stood, both braves and horses alike,

in line along the bluff's edge, feathers snapping in the stiff breeze, war paint glistening in the sun, scanning the vastness that lay before them, their domain, with their right hands shading their eyes, except of course the Chief, because of his deformed crooked index finger, he'd surely poke himself in the eye if he tried it. But then, he was the Chief; his job was only to evaluate and act upon the information as it was fed to him. Patiently he waited; then, finally, the first report was relayed to him from the seismic system. Left Ear had scored.

Once deciphered, the report clearly indicated that the disturbance was now coming from due west from where they stood and that now familiar sounds could also be distinguished, such as squeaky wheels, animal hooves and foot steps co-mingled with the unidentifiable rumbling shockwaves no doubt being generated by freight wagons bearing heavy cargo (bells and barrels), as well as human voices, but of an unfamiliar nature, unlike the foul-mouthed, aggressive, profanity-punctuated, tobacco-chewing cattlemen and pioneers they had encountered in the past.

No sooner had the seismic report been relayed and deciphered, the visual surveillance team relayed their report to the Chief setting forth their findings in lengthy detail. The report stated that, according to the wagon tracks deeply imprinted in the desert floor below along with crushed sagebrush along the way, heavily laden freight wagons as well as covered wagons had passed that way. And that apparently there'd been an encampment of sorts as indicated by a clearing of sagebrush, however left in a fashion and manor not consistent to white man practices whereas tin cans, bottles, discarded furniture or wagon parts and trash in general would be left strewn helter skelter all over Hell's Creation. The report also stated that there appears to be a fairly large mound of freshly disturbed earth materials with a wooden cross implanted on it, that if it were not for its configuration and size, it could be construed as a grave. There was no explanation for this, and neither was there an explanation for the fact that the caravan was, in their opinion, off course, since the established California trail was further South, and the Oregon trail was more to the North. Whoever these people were, they were either lost or blazing a new trail, which was not to their liking.

Satisfied with the reports, the Chief ordered an end to surveillance by both the below and the above intelligence gathering system. The War Council was now called into session. They would now contemplate their next move.

CHAPTER 13

Surrounded by his War Staff, Chief Crooked Finger proceeded to apprize them of the findings and upon doing so, asked for their input. Amongst hand gestures, grunts and inarticulate wailing, at times high pitched exclamations punctuated with the waving of war staffs, it finally boiled down to how far could the perpetrators get before sundown and could they catch up to them this day. The logical answer lay with Left Ear. But when asked, he did not step forward, simply because he was not amongst them. This fact became quite obvious since he was still stuck to the rock some dozen or so yards from where the meeting was taking place. After several calls to him, lacking a response, the Chief reined his horse up to Left Ear, berated him for not terminating surveillance as ordered and not being present at the meeting. His final comment was:

"Get over here!"

Without giving his official tracker the opportunity to explain the reason for his disobedience, he jabbed his horse in the belly with his war staff which set the animal at a fast trot back to the Council. The truth of the matter was, considering that the rock outcropping's base extended some thousand feet down and below the desert floor, which made it possible for it to intercept the horizontally traveling seismic sound waves being generated from several miles distance, then rearrange them by bending them ninety degrees in order to set them on the vertical course of which by doing so, friction at the bend coupled with the pronounced pull of gravity since the sound waves were now traveling up hill

Dago Red! Westward - Ho!

to an elevation of as much as one thousand feet, a tremendous strain had been put on Left Ear's left ear, to the extent that the extra degree of vacuum applied to draw the sound waves to the brain not only securely sucked his ear tight to the smooth rock surface, but also shifted the entire contents of his cranium, including the intricate structure of the inner ear of his right ear, towards that side of the head thus rendering him stone deaf in his right ear. Finally through his hand gestures and garbled pleadings, a couple of braves did surmise that he was in fact in need of assistance, and so they sped to his aid.

Upon analyzing their comrade's predicament, and applying their knowledge of basic physics, primarily "what goes up must come down," they concluded that once the demand ceased, the sound waves reversed themselves thus causing a horrendous vacuum void as they plunged back down the vertical whence they came. Atmospheric pressure being what it is even at those higher elevations, and considering that an ear the size of Left Ear's (about the size of an average toilet plunger), atmospheric forces on the outside of the ear, in their attempt to fill the sudden void within the ear caused by the vacuum, exerted so much pressure that it was plastering the hapless victim's head up against the rock's surface tighter than a buffalo bull's ass at fly time.

They therefore concluded that the vacuum must be broken in order to extricate him. They tried pulling his head back off the rock, but then realized that they were in fact aggravating the problem. The idea was abandoned lest the contents of his cranium would surely be sucked into the ear. After several other attempts, a simple solution was formulated. By forcing the blade of their tomahawks between the ear and the rock, they broke the vacuum, thus causing their comrade's head to bounce back with a loud "POP." The sudden surge within the cranium to re-establish its contents back to rightful positions all but knocked Left Ear to the ground. Staggering like a drunken sailor, in a zig-zag pattern and syncopated gait, he made it back to the Council and, for what it was worth, prepared himself to add his expertise to the problem at hand. So, short and to the point questions were put to him, and with nature's resilient power of recovery returning his brain cells back to their normal configuration, answered the questions in a like manner:

"What kind of people?"
"Don't know."
"How fast travel?"
"Slow."
"How far now?"

This question required a gesture; arm and hand pointing straight up to indicate the sun at exactly Midday, then lowering it to a given point towards the West. The answer:

"Four hours by horse."
"Maybe make camp?"
"Yes."

Being near sunset, it was logical that the perpetrators would make camp and equally logical that they should not pursue them at this time. The squabble amongst themselves as to their next move escalated whereas those in favor of at least investigating the supposed grave site before returning back to their camp won out.

Taking full command, the Chief organized the braves into a single file column with himself riding point, with the Platoon Commander directly behind him, and Left Ear taking up the rear, and since he was still somewhat wobbly he was followed by the Medicine Man for he was now considered a casualty and could collapse most any time. Right arm outstretched in the direction they must go, crooked index finger correctly but unintentionally pointing over the edge of the bluff, the Chief ordered the column to move out.

Jabbing their war staffs into the ribs of their mounts, they streamed over the edge winding their way down the steep south side of the plateau to the desert floor below. There, they regrouped, the Chief taking center lead position, flanked equally on both sides by his eager braves. Horses at ready, he gave the final order:

"Charge! Display your courage to the Spirits of the Mountain!"

In a display of determination, the steeds bolted forward. Having experienced this sort of thing before, the riders leaned into it while clasping a handful of mane lest they be flipped backwards and left afoot because in no way would their steeds wait for them. They'd stay with the rest, regardless.

Once on the straightaway, the horses broke out into full frenzied gallop. Charging through sagebrush, manes and tails to the breeze, they carried their war-whooping riders towards their quarry. The Chief himself leading the charge, a figure of courage and leadership the likes as never seen before, feathers from his headgear snapping in the wind, as did the feathers at the end of his war staff being held in his left hand, pointing and aiming directly at the quarry, while his right arm was held high gyrating, his hand with the crooked index finger forever jerking upwards as if giving Satan himself the finger, screamed:

"Onward! Onward! Kill or be killed! Take no prisoners!" With war whoops and hollers, the hysterical braves acknowledged the command.

Not entirely sure as to the purpose or urgency of their campaign, the horses, hooves clattering, ears pinned back, fierce frenzied eyes even more so than their masters', their frothing mouths and flared nostrils, along with their masters' appearance, was enough to scare the Living Demons out of the Devil himself and the Gargoyles off the Steeples of Hell. From the viewpoint of their objective, this oncoming juggernaut as a whole took on the appearance of an approaching one-hundred-mile-an-hour hurricane of sorts, crushing and uprooting everything in its path and leaving nothing but a cloud of dust in its wake.

However, as fierce as these warriors may be, upon reaching the supposed mysterious grave site's outer boundary, if in fact it were such, they pulled their mounts up short amidst a scattering of dirt. They were indeed the bravest of braves in dealing with their counterparts on a man-to-man basis, but now, who amongst them was prepared to take on the spirits of the unknown? While they remained mounted on their sweaty, panting steeds, they pondered the question. As with Brazilian tree frogs during their mating season on refreshing rainy nights, all remained silent until the first dared speak, then once one broke silence they all chimed in in a conglomeration of wailing jabber, each trying to induce the other into stepping forward and testing the waters. But since the Spirits of the dead could very well be involved, no one dared volunteer. So it was now up to the Chief to appoint the most likely person best adapted for the job, and who might that be? Once again, Left Ear.

Why? Because he put up the least resistance since his horse hadn't caught up to the others in time to get in on the full discussions, and therefore didn't really know what it was all about. His horse had been slowed down due to the imbalance of Left Ear's head. His left ear, having swollen to unbelievable proportions due to the aforementioned ordeal back at the rock, was causing him to lean heavily to port side, thus causing the horse to compensate for the unbalanced load by listing heavily to starboard, lest both mount and mounted fall over on their sides. Aside from that fact, in truth, he was the best qualified since with his ear to the mound, it might just be possible to detect what else might be buried there besides a corpse, if in fact there even was a corpse as the cross made up of barrel staves might indicate.

Therefore while the others stood around at a safe distance, Left Ear cautiously crept up to the mound of dirt and let his left ear drop in a free fall. Once dust and debris had settled down within the cavity of his ear from the sudden plunging disturbance, an interesting unusual sound coming from beneath the mound was detected, a dripping sound.

Satisfied that the mound may not in fact be a grave containing a corpse, and therefore Spirits, evil or otherwise, may not be an issue, the rest of the tribe gathered around the mound and once again engaged in oratory debate:

"To dig or not to dig?"

Resolved that Spirits did not give off such sounds, and therefore no harm would come to them, they unanimously agreed to dig.

Ignoring the markings on the cross (Giuseppe Giovanni/ MDCCL-MDCCCL), they pulled the barrel staves apart and using them for shovels, proceeded to dig out the contents of this curious mound of dirt that was emitting dripping sounds, of all places, underground.

Although he was not about to interfere, the Medicine Man remained skeptical, especially of the markings on the cross not being consistent with common English, of which he did have some knowledge.

The braves dug furiously. Within minutes they'd uncovered what was now obvious, an oak barrel. "But why would anyone want to bury a plain water barrel?" so they thought. Chief Crooked Finger was devastated with the find. All that military strategy applied and time expended, just for that? Certainly he'd be the laughing stock of the whole of the Indian community West of the Mississippi. However, as the others argued and bitched, the Medicine Man, the wise one, while scratching his chin, studied the situation with interest. Here was this barrel, with its bung being tightly hammered in place, although covered with soil, extending only partially below the surface. A cross with strange markings, no doubt the name of the deceased, date of birth and death, thus indicating a possible burial. "There's got to be more," he thought. The Chief, noting that the wise one was in deep thought, then suddenly seeing him plunge his hand into his bag of tricks, then retrieving it with a handful of assorted bones of a prairie dog, and then, tossing them onto the ground, inquisitively asked:

"What do you make of it?"

"Look, see the formation of the bones?" instructed the wise one. Not to appear an idiot to the rest of them who by now fell silent, the Chief responded:

"Yes . . . yes, I see them, and . . .?"

"You notice how they point?" interrupted the wise one.

"Yes . . I see it . . . I see it," answered the Chief eagerly.

By now they were all gathered around staring at the bones, obviously, like the Chief, not seeing what the Medicine Man saw. In unison, puzzled, they looked from the bones to the Medicine Man questionably. Without asking it, they got an answer along with instructions.

"More below, dig deeper."

"Where?"

"There, where hear drip," said the wise one pointing to the base of the barrel head. With the barrel still nesting comfortably in its original position, they scratched around until they exposed the spigot of which extended a hollow cane from its spout straight down deeper into the earth below. In addition to the now pronounced dripping sound, sweet, aromatic, but intoxicating, vapors wafted up thus exciting their smell sensing membranes to the point of ecstacy.

Dago Red! Westward - Ho!

They crowded around even closer, each trying to sniff and suck in as much of the vapors as possible. The pushing and shoving that ensued brought about a strict command:

"Back off! Damn it!" ordered the Chief, then added as if it were he that first discovered this miracle so divine:

"Medicine Man, I commission you to carefully analyze our discovery," he said with a pleading expression in hopes that his wise man could give him a hint as to where to go from here. And so the wise man stated again, adding caution to his statement:

"Dig deeper, where hear drip, follow cane, careful," advised the Medicine Man.

And so they eagerly but carefully dug deeper until they finally hit wood, a more or less flat surface made up of barrel staves. By now the pleasant but intoxicating fumes wafting up from this entire conglomeration of barrel, spigot, cane tube, and up through the cracks of the rearranged barrel staves was driving them into a frenzy.

Like so many warthogs, with bare hands, tomahawks and whatever else they could muster up, careful not to cause a shifting or damage to this mysterious apparatus, dug around and down until they had a pit the size of an average concert hall. Looking from a short distance, aside from the horses standing around, the Chief in all his feathered splendor, and the Medicine Man fiddling with lizard skins, frog skeletons, braids of crow feet as he studied the markings on the cross stave of the cross, all you could see was dirt ejecting from the pit with an occasional head bobbing up for a breath of fresh air.

However once they started to clear the earth materials from around the apparatus below, it suddenly became obvious that this was a coffin, made up of barrel staves. Tempered by the intoxicating fumes they'd ingested was the one single factor that kept them from stampeding to their horses and riding the hell out of there lest the spirits of the dead overtake their souls. All but a few remained in the pit and only because they were so intoxicated they couldn't crawl out.

Once again the Chief, by now also a little tipsy, as was his Medicine Man, standing there fumbling with his trinkets, turned to the wise man for further guidance. A question and answer conversation between them ensued:

"Why coffin make mysterious Good Spirit?" asked the Chief.

"Spirit not from coffin. Come from barrel," came the answer.

"From water barrel?"

"Not water barrel. No water in barrel."

"No water? Then what is it? White Man trick?"

"No trick. No White Man."

With this the wise one pointed out the markings not only on the stave he was holding, but also on the barrel head that were obviously not in English. He did conclude that the barrel stave cross gave the name of the person buried there but he was baffled by the Roman numerals as was he with the similar inscribed format of stampings on the barrel head that indicated its capacity, the maker of the barrel, the date it was made and by whom, and its contents: "Vino."

He also noted that the barrel was made of heavier and of different design and workmanship than the water barrels used by the pioneers. The Chief was getting impatient and so expressed his feelings:

"Damn it! I don't want to know what's not in the barrel or who's not in the coffin, or inscriptions you don't understand, so tell me . . ." Before finishing the sentence, remembering what his wife told him that set them on this journey in the first place, glanced towards the Medicine Man, noticed him working his fingers along a string of bones made up from the spine of a weasel (with an occasional interruption of

Dago Red! Westward - Ho!

the beak of a raven), he blurted:

"Quit fiddling around and get your damned butt down there and find out what the hell this is all about!"

Put out that he, a man of such a highly regarded profession, should be addressed in such a derogatory manner, let fly a derogatory response of his own, while violently shaking the rattles of a rattlesnake to let the Gods know of the Chief's unorthodox behavior, he scurried down into the pit, ordered the lid ripped off the coffin, and upon so doing, everyone gasped at the sight that lay before their eyes.

There, lying on his back with a smile and tranquil look on his face, fresh rosy complexion, eyes open as well as mouth receiving the drops of liquid from the barrel above, lay what appeared to be more alive than dead, the corpse of a man. Unbeknownst to them, they had just discovered a makeshift tomb of a true Etruscan, an Italian, a Capo no less, adhering to the traditions of ancient Etruria, the origin of his clan, the Paradise of Italy, where flowed an abundance of wine, the nectar of life, the catalyst of love. And where dwelled both Bacchus and Eros, the Roman Gods of wine and love, to instill in the minds of its inhabitants the importance of: "to live and let live, to love and be loved!"

And now, having lived no less than 100 years, twice a widower, married three times, sired six children by each of his three wives, the youngest being Giuseppina, born to his present wife, Maria, some forty years his junior, now lying there embalmed with wine, he was taking his most precious treasure (wine) with him to the Promised Land. And little did the Indians know that, being a caravan made up of Italians, devout Catholics, true believers if you will, as long as they had bread and wine (of which they had an abundance), the symbol of body and blood amongst Christians, the basic ingredients to perform their religious ceremonies, the Good Lord would guide and look after them. So never at any time could they be lost. As for the seismic vibrations, it was this fact, oxen drawn freight wagons heavily laden with barrel upon barrel of wine, giving off intense rumbling vibrations as they trudged along on uneven terrain, that brought about the phenomenon.

    The Medicine Man without further ado, and certainly not waiting for any further instruction from the irate Chief, turned off the flow of the eternal gift of life (wine), removed the hollow cane, placed a dehydrated, in full plume, wing of an eagle across the face of the corpse, thus sending his soul in full flight escorted by the Spirits of Eternity, to the Promised Land as they, the Indians, knew it, then repeatedly mumbling prayers understood only by their own Gods, ordered the tomb restored and re-buried with the exception of the wine barrel, which they rolled up on a mound of dirt, placed it in the same position as it previously was, only now well elevated. The Medicine Man, now acting more like a religious man, reconstructed the cross to its original configuration and planted it back in its appropriate position.

    As much as they would have liked to, hauling the near full barrel back to camp was deemed to be impractical and, therefore, out of the question. Although they knew not what this liquid was or where it may have come from, they were convinced that its consumption would no doubt not only make them feel good, unlike the firewater acquired from the fur traders that sent them into crazed convulsions, but instead, was sure to give them Eternal Life whether it be on Earth or where the Spirits dwelled. The deep rich, red color of the wine led them to believe that this was the blood of their Savior, be he of red skin, white, black, yellow or olive complexioned God or otherwise, made little difference for blood is blood, and without it, there is no life. Thus, in a brawling manner, they argued the fate of the contents of the barrel. To the last man, they voted unanimously to consume the contents there and then lest the Spirits, their Gods, never forgive them for wasting their blood needlessly.

However, the problem now was, since they had no utensils of sorts with them to dispense the wine equally among themselves, just how could they ration it equally? Obviously they turned to the Chief for the answer who, in turn, turned to the Medicine Man (apologetically), the wise one, to apply his scientific and mathematical skills to solve this intricate problem.

Within seconds the ingenious mind of the Medicine Man came up with the answer, and so advised the Chief by way of hand gestures, expressions and grunts.

Realizing that his wise man was still somewhat PO'd at him, the Chief, in an abnormal display of respect, so advised the others that he, the Medicine Man, was fully in charge of the dispensing of the contents of the barrel. Accepting the assignment, orders were issued in military fashion, blunt and to the point:

All personnel fall in!"

Within an instant a line formed at attention. Considering their somewhat intoxicated, tipsy condition from inhaling wine fumes, it was orderly. The Chief was impressed; he'd selected the right man for the job. The braves eagerly waited for the next order:

"Present scrotums!"

As quick as one could say: "Cock Robin," antelope skin shorts dropped below the knees exposing about the most ridiculous array of balls imaginable. The Chief was astounded as was the Medicine Man for it was not intended that they present their scrotums per se, but rather, the buffalo scrotums they carried their rations in. Immediately the order was retracted and a new order issued:

"Present buffalo scrotum pouches!"

Now this made sense. A third order followed:

"Discard contents!"

With that order, scraps of coyote meat, grasshoppers, beetles, marinated raven gizzards, roasted acorns and a few freshly caught horned toad lizards were strewn about. The final order:

"Left face, march!"

With that order, the Medicine Man took the lead, marched up to the barrel and proceeded to fill the buffalo scrotum pouches from its contents. The Chief followed by Left Ear took up the rear of the column. Not until they'd been served did the Medicine Man fill his own scrotum. As efficiently as a Basque drinking wine from his bota, they eagerly drank the wine from their scrotums.

The process continued throughout the evening until finally the barrel was empty. By then the braves were really stoned, staggering about in the moonlight, stumbling and falling as they laughed and howled at the moon. To the coyotes that inhabited the land, they interpreted this as an encroachment on their territory, therefore they howled back. The more the braves howled, the more the coyotes howled. The more the coyotes howled, the more the braves howled for they now had found a new God, such as the Romans had done when they found Bacchus, the Roman God of Wine. They, too, howled throughout the night, and did so for many moons thereafter.

With somewhat regained composure, Chief Crooked Finger finally retook command. With slurred speech, he made the announcement, followed by an order:

"The party's over! Mount your horses and let's go home!"

Once mounted and draped upon their horses, hanging onto a fistful of mane, horse sense came into play. Pitch dark or moonlight, the horses need not be prodded or reined for they knew what was expected of them, and mainly, they knew the way home.

Dago Red! Westward - Ho!

CHAPTER 14

Arriving back in camp in the wee hours of the morning, the braves loosened their grips on the manes and dropped to the ground. Greeted by the dogs who were still guarding the coyote carcass, but with no desire to be lambasted by their squaws for being drunk, the braves slept where they dropped amongst the dogs to wait out the dawn and the hangover that was sure to come.

By mid-morning they began to stir, but to their surprise, they had no hangover such as they'd experienced after a bout with firewater. As a matter of fact, they felt better now than the morning before. And, to their surprise, they found themselves sexually stimulated all due to the consumption of the contents of the barrel clearly stamped: "Vino." However, suspicious of their husbands' sudden interest in sex, their husbands' discovery soon became known to the wives. Once the secret was out that during their campaign the day before, their braves had indeed discovered the secret of longevity and sexual potency. Without bothering to hear the details, the wives demanded that they share this nectar of life with them as well, and if in fact their scrotums were now empty, that they go back out and fill them up again and bring them back full, or else! And, in the meantime, they'd not share in the porcupine they had shaken out of a pine tree and clubbed to death, unless they wanted to eat it raw since they'd not put it on the spit for roasting. And that they, their husbands, would be barred from their wigwam permanently, unless a genuine promise was made to do the aforesaid, pronto!

As for retaliation, the braves might just as well forget about it because the squaws did all the work anyway, so there was nothing to retaliate with. So rather than argue the issue, the Council went into session to hash over the prospects of overtaking the bearers of the nectar of life, wine, and get them to divulge the location of the spring that gave forth this gift of life. And while they were at it, learn more about their God Bacchus (name yet unknown to them) since all their own Gods ever did for them was raise havoc with their thunder and lightning strikes.

Upon adjourning the session, the Council made the announcement that they'd pursue the matter post haste. This, obviously, pleased their wives; they'd have roasted porcupine for dinner that evening. And of course, this also pleased the dogs since now the coyote carcass would be discarded and left to their disposal.

Time was short, evening would soon be upon them, signalmen were launched into action. On a knoll above camp, signal fires were now smouldering ready to send forth smoke signals. The Chief, accompanied by his key men, the Medicine Man and Left Ear, took a position with a clear view of a plateau in the distance, due West. The signalmen, wet blanket in hand, awaited the order to set the wireless, silent, coded, most efficient transcontinental relay communication system ever devised into action. Directed to his brother-in-law, Chief Freeloader (so named due to his habit of forever inviting himself to dinner but never reciprocating), correspondence commenced:

"Urgent, be alerted!" read the puffs of smoke drifting skyward.
"Gotcha, what's for dinner?" came the immediate response.
"Five day old coyote!"
"If that's it, forget it. Can't come."
"Fine! Stay put! Need surveillance!"
"Gotcha, what's up?"

Dago Red! Westward - Ho!

"Watch for caravan, mysterious people!"

"What for?"

"Never mind what for, just watch for them!"

The Chief didn't want to let on the purpose lest his brother-in-law would muscle in on their find. The smoke signals continued:

"All right. Which way are they traveling?"

The signalmen, as with many people of different ethnic backgrounds, had difficulty with the "th's" and the "r's," so the answer to the asked question read:

"Da-go . . . West?"

"Affirmative. Will advise upon arrival."

A string of smoke puffs from both signal stations signified an over and out close.

The Chief now turned to his official tracker, Left Ear. With his keen sense of sound and vibrations, hopefully he could pinpoint exactly where the caravan was camped, and their chances of catching up with them the next day.

"Where camp now? Where camp next rising moon?" asked the Chief with one arm outstretched Easterly towards the rising moon and the other Westerly towards the assumed direction of the caravan.

Plopping his ear to the ground, distant vibrations instantly filtered through the sensing mechanism of his massive ear. With absolute certainty he was able to distinguish and screen the different seismic vibrations that not only told him that this was unquestionably the same caravan that he was now locked in on, but also, their step-by-step activities at the moment and pinpoint their exact location by the various natural sounds surrounding the encampment being transformed into vibrations. While still plastered to the ground, he relayed his findings:

"Much music. Like whistling wind in cathedral rocks and pine trees. Many feet stomping, laughter, singing like birds in springtime." Being Italians, and Saturday night at that, what he was hearing was concertina, guitars, mandolins, piccolo and the violin pounding out old Italian folk songs, and of course, singing and dancing the Tarantella, thus following the old Roman traditions (however short of an outright "orgy") in honor of Bacchus and Dionysus (God and Goddess of Wine) with the little rascal Eros (God of Love) with his bow and arrow standing by ready to pierce the hearts of those who took liberties with their sexual emotions.

"Wait! I sense mysterious rumbling vibrations like many rocks crashing together!" he announced. These vibrations were not the same mysterious rumblings of wine barrels during transport that he'd heard before. What he was now sensing was two Bocce Ball Courts, side by side, in action. Apparently the Italians planned to stay awhile.

"All right, all right! But where are they?"

"East bank of River Snake!!" The way it was said indicated something troublesome.

"River Snake!!" exclaimed the Chief. "What the hell?? Quick, get my brother-in-law back on line!" he ordered.

The signalmen flew into action. Within minutes, Chief Freeloader was again on line. Puffs of smoke drifted upward in the twilight evening, sending forth a lengthy message, which was also being monitored by the Chief's daughter-in-law, Two-Dove's, father, Chief Lame Duck (so named because he was useless as a leader since his wife sat in on the council meetings and made all the decisions for him) who was camped to the East and who had it in for the Chief because the wampum paid for his daughter's hand in marriage to the Chief's son, Two Dog, turned out to be counterfeit. And so he eavesdropped with growing interest.

"Caravan in question on East Bank of River Snake! Must hold them there at all costs! Caravan must not be allowed to attempt crossing River Snake, Urgent!!" read the message.

Dago Red! Westward - Ho!

"Sorry pal. I'm on the West Side. No way will we cross River Snake this time of year!!" The return message was just as urgently expressed.

"Damn it!" swore the Chief, then, wih expressed concern, addressed the Medicine Man:

"Medicine Man, you know the consequences if . . ." Pausing for an instant with a look of horror, he continued:

"Do something! Anything! But quick!"

This was indeed a tall order but, luckily, the Medicine Man had his ritual bag with him, a well cured belly of a buffalo. Scavenging through its contents, he came up with the needed ingredients to do the job, to get the attention of the Spirits, for only they could do what needed to be done on such short notice. From the belly bag, he retrieved three buffalo scrotum pouches. One contained finely ground charcoal, the other sulfur, and the third one, potassium nitrate, acquired such as the sulfur from a strata outcropping of a hot pit in the middle of the desert that they referred to as the "Devils Throat" since it would at times belch forth bursts of hot, slimy goo, choking gases and an occasional blast of multi-colored flame.

He now ordered everyone to step back a safe distance from the signal fire, then planted his medicine staff, with its array of feathers, into the ground on the side facing the mountain to the East where dwelled the Spirits. He now emptied the rest of the contents from the ritual bag onto the ground. Well back from the signal fire, he carefully poured the contents from the three scrotum pouches into the bag while mixing them thoroughly. No doubt the most powerful magical ritual was about to be launched. The Chief, as well as all the others, with the exception of Left Ear who was still at his post some dozen yards from where the ritual would take place, stood trembling with awe, for they sensed that this one would, surely, be the big one.

Poised at the signal fire, the Medicine Man reached into the ritual bag, took a pinch of the mixed substance and tossed it into the fire causing a flare up and minor explosion of sorts. As the flash of flame burst upward, he pranced around the fire uttering high-pitched sounds, and as he came around to where he'd jabbed the staff into the ground, tossed more substance into the fire, thus emitting an even more intense explosion and higher burst of flames while at the same instant, thrust his arm straight at the mountain to the East while exerting a fierce but pleading expression with added escalated chantings directed to the Spirits that dwelled there. Again and again, always with escalated frenzy, he repeated the procedure until finally, a flash of lightning followed by rumbling thunder came forth from the mountain.

He'd gotten the attention of the Spirits of the Mountain. Now, pointing due West, applying all the energy he could muster, with blood-curdling exclamations, high pitched wailings that sent coyotes running for cover, he apprized the Spirits of the situation, and to: "Save the caravan from the horrors of River Snake!" In a final frenzied stampede around the fire, he slammed the ritual pouch with its contents of magical powers into the fire, thus creating one last horrendous explosion that sent an enormous tower of flames reaching ever skyward. With that, the plains fell silent. Never before had such a display of Spiritual Power been witnessed.

Suddenly, to the East, smoke signals spiraled upwards from Chief Lame Duck's own signal station. With a tinge of sarcasm, it read:

"Now you've done it! You crooked jerk!" Then followed by:

"May the wrath of the Spirits rain havoc upon you . . . you . . . wampum counterfeiting son-of-a-scorpion!"

"Up your ass . . . sucker! Hang up! This is none of your business!" responded the Chief indignantly. Chief Lame

Dago Red! Westward - Ho!

Duck would be the last one he'd want horning in on this deal.

Some fifteen or so miles West on the West Bank of the River Snake, the Chief's brother-in-law along with a handful of braves stood in awe at the display of flashes that intermittently lit up the sky to the East, and then the final high flash that lit up the skies for miles around, reaching clear up to the heavens above, then followed by the venom punctuated conversation between his brother-in-law and Chief Lame Duck. In amazement he commented:

"Holy smokes! Look at that! My brother-in-law's Medicine Man has blown his stack! Chief Lame Duck is right! There'll be hell to pay tonight!" exclaimed Chief Freeloader.

Within seconds of the statement being made, a series of powerful strikes of lightening generated from a sudden formation of dark clouds crashed into the mountain range to the North, the headwaters of the River Snake. Along with the flashes, a barrage of thunder echoed across the land, and between the two, sending seismic and aerial shockwaves surging in all directions, shattering rock formations in their path. Left Ear, the tracker, still at his post, was caught completely off guard, thus the sudden powerful surge of seismic vibrations bounced him up off the ground, momentarily rendering him senseless, thus sending him staggering through the sagebrush in a complete state of confusion.

The above-ground sound waves all but flattened the Chief, the Medicine Man and the signal crew, scattered horses into a stampede, and sent the dogs ky-yi-ing in wild confusion.

To the West, torrents of rain poured onto the mountain range the likes of which had not been seen since Noah's Ark, instantly flooding the creeks and gullies that fed the River Snake. Surges of storm waters choked with debris came crashing down the mountainside and into the main river channel. The flash flood, a wall of water some 50 feet high carrying mud, logs and rocks the size of tombstones, came thundering down the gorge, sweeping it clean down to bedrock. Luckily for the encampments, Chief Freeloader's on the West Bank and the Italians' on the East Bank of the river, they were well above the high water mark for as the front of this wall of devastation swept by, if not millions, certainly thousands of venomous deadly snakes, Water Moccasins no less, the scourge of the River Snake, in a churning frenzied state of destruction, were being crushed to death and swept onto the hot, dry desert floor where the waters of the river are absorbed into the sand, thus leaving whatever survivors of those water-dependent venomous creatures there may be, to perish in the scorching sands of the desert.

Dago Red! Westward - Ho!

CHAPTER 15

Next morning at the crack of dawn, the braves once again were mounted on their steeds and ready to move out. However this time their scrotum pouches contained fresh sliced roasted porcupine marinated in grasshopper sauce. The coyote carcass had been flung out into the sagebrush where a fierce battle now raged between the dogs and a band of coyotes in a winner-take-all struggle for possession. And of all things, the battle encompassed the route the braves must take heading West, meaning that they must guide their horses through the midst of these rampant, ravaging beasts.

However, this time it was noted that the Chief was taking along his ornately-feathered Calumet, the pipe of peace, along with a scrotum of salt. After all, one never knows, in event of a turn of events whereas defeat is inevitable, the next best thing is to sue for peace, and there's nothing better than the sharing of a puff of smoke and pinch of salt to seal a peace treaty.

And once again the matter of his son, the one-day heir to his throne, Two Dog, was not among the mounted. Knowing their responsibility, without the official order to do so, two braves dismounted and pranced toward Two Dog's wigwam with the intent of dragging him out bare-assed-naked if need be. Without giving thought to what was going on under the blankets, they grabbed up the entire bedding configuration and, since the newlyweds were locked up in sexual embrace, dragged both occupants out into the campsite. The Chief, indignant and cursing, promptly addressed the situation:

"Stop!" he ordered. "Drag them back to the wigwam."
Then in a fit of rage, cursed:
"Damned those f___ dogs the day he was born. And damned those double crossers up on the mountain for they not only cursed my son but also cursed my daughter-in-law, Two Dove, as well. And to make it even worse, he paired them. Now look what we've got!" Hesitating for an instant, a more pleasant thought crossed his mind:
"Well, I guess a dozen or so grandchildren running around camp might not be all that bad after all."
The two braves, having carried out their orders, came trotting back expressing sheepish grins. The Chief noticed and commented:
"What's with you two?" he asked.
"Two Dog - Two Dove, never missed a stroke," they answered gleefully. No doubt they were so engrossed in their lovemaking, and being locked up such as they were, they never even realized they'd been dragged in and out of the wigwam. Shaking his head in disbelief, and resolved to the futility of ever making a warrior out of his sex-crazed son, the Chief gave the order to move out.
The route out of camp took them in the direction of the on-going battle between dogs and coyotes. Although by now the roasted coyote carcass they'd been fighting over was torn to shreds, scattered in bits and pieces throughout the sagebrush, made little difference to their desire to fight.
Amidst their tooth gnashing, snarling, growling and occasional ky-yi and yips of pain, the war party paused to view this bedlam of cartwheeling canines battling to the death. The Medicine Man, being an authority on just about anything dealing with the health and well being of man, beast or, for that matter, the Spirits, felt it in order to advise the Chief of the possible consequences of this carnage they were witnessing. In brief, he said:

Dago Red! Westward - Ho!

"Better stop fight. Maybe coyote kill dogs." The comment had merit since the coyotes outnumbered the dogs.

But the Chief, after giving it a little thought, responded nonchalantly, also in brief:

"Fine, coyote kill dog, we eat dog." Of course, this comment had merit also since the dogs were by far better eating than the coyotes.

With a wave of hand and shrug of shoulder, the Chief signaled to move on and leave the dogs to their own fate. As it was his job to do so, since he was the official tracker and knew the exact direction they must go, Left Ear took the lead.

About the time they'd topped the ridge to the West of camp where by now the sounds of the raging coyote carcass battle echoing up from below could no longer be heard, the sun rose behind them. The sun's rays glistened off the bony features of the Chief, giving him the appearance of an old dried out tree snag as he followed the lead man, Left Ear, whose head, from the rear, took on the appearance of a melon with a trumpet stuck through it, the mushroom button shaped cupped mouthpiece protruding out the right side and the flared, funnel-shaped bell out the left side. Following the Chief, the Medicine Man with all his gadgetry dangling about him, adorned with bleached bones and multicolored feathers, and several snake skins, complete with rattles attached, thus sending off maracas-like musical sounds while floating in the breeze, except for the absence of pots and pans, looked like a vendor at a state fair. Behind the leaders, moving along in single file, war paint reflecting off their semi-naked bodies and faces, more so with their commander appearing to have been smeared with red lipstick in a fashion that gave the impression he'd been besieged by a contingency of over-sexed whores, the warriors followed grimly for when it came time to do battle, they'd be the ones pushed to the front.

They made their way down the slope and onto the desert floor where they now moved briskly along in a somewhat disorganized group, crossing the better part of the remaining ten or so miles to the base of a rise that shielded their approach to the supposed encampment of these mysterious people on the other side where the River Snake flowed. Upon arriving at the base, they paused. The Chief requested the time of day from the Medicine Man. Glancing up at the position of the sun, then to his shadow cast on the ground, the Medicine Man announced the precise time of day. It was two minutes before the hour of 10:00 o'clock a.m. Central Time.

"Good, we've made good time," said the Chief. "We will rest our horses for a few minutes while Left Ear gauges the exact distance to our quarry's encampment. Dismount!" he ordered. Assuming it to be an order, Left Ear slid off his horse and plunked his ear to the ground while the others milled around waiting for further orders.

But they were not the only ones heading West to intercept the Italians. John, having reached the fork in the trail the day before and seeing that the caravan carrying his loved one had in fact either misinterpreted or ignored the Colonel's instructions and warnings, thus as indicated were now heading into forbidden territory, left him in a panic. With complete disregard for his own well being, he reined his horse on course with the newly blazed trail and by jabbing him in the flanks with his spurs let it be known that time was of the essence. Still in the saddle after dark, by the light of the full moon he picked his way until by sunup he'd arrived at the burial site. The markings on the cross sadly told him in an instant who was buried there.

John's sorrow soon turned to horror and anger as he viewed the many horses' hoof prints and moccasined footprints in the soft, freshly disturbed soil. He swore: "Damn those Indians! Surely they've done 'em all in!"

Dago Red! Westward - Ho!

Having said that, reins in hand, he walked circling out further and further, dreading the thought of what he might find. In so doing, he found nothing tangible but did notice something of interest. The wagon tracks leading away from the scene were clear of any horse prints or moccasined footprints. Working his way back following the tracks left by the heavy wine wagon, he again came across hoof and moccasin prints, but did notice that they overlayed the wagon tracks. It was obvious: the Indians had appeared on the scene after the caravan had left.

In excitement and with pounding heart he exclaimed:
"Thank God! They didn't pursue them!"
But then a sudden thought crashed through his mind:
"Why? Why didn't they go after the caravan? All these tracks are fresh."
The thought triggered another disturbing thought:
"They'll ambush them further up the line. Yes! That's it! Damn it, I wonder how far out they are?"
Moving around to the right side of his horse, he jerked the Winchester out of its scabbard, pumped a shell from the magazine into the firing chamber, emptied a box of shells into his pockets, then talking directly to his horse as if he were a person, stated:
"We've got to get moving fast. Those bastards know the lay of the land, and if we drag our feet, we'll be too late."
Setting the rifle's hammer down to its safe position, he slammed it back into its scabbard, ran around to the left side and swung himself into the saddle as he again addressed his mount, only this time with a screaming command:
"Yaa . . . Yaa . . .! Go, damn it! We still have a chance!"
With Giuseppina heavy on his mind, he spurred his horse into full gallop. The terrain being flat and sagebrush sparse, with the rider's motions synchronized to the steed's galloping gait, the miles shrank to mere yards.

Meanwhile, on the other side of the rise at the encampment, the bell boys were standing by to pull the rope that bonged the huge cast bronze bell attached to its yoke, suspended across a high tripod of poles. This was Sunday morning and at the exact time of 10:00 o'clock a.m., the bonging of the bell would signify the start of Mass of which all of these God-fearing Italian Catholic worshipers must attend or be forever condemned to Hell's Damnation.

And of course, since Reverend Gadwall had, in order to stay with the wine wagon, conned the Italians into accepting him as a priest at least for the interim, he'd be expected to conduct the saying of Mass of which he knew nothing about. Besides, ever since he'd taken up with the Italian caravan, he'd spent all of his time standing by the wine spigot thus becoming the self-appointed Official Dispenser. However, to not over indulge in the wine, he did adhere to his strict policy of never drinking unless he was alone or with somebody. So, needless to say, whatever time of day or night it was, he was always in a state of inebriety.

This particular Sunday morning was no exception. Brazen as a peacock in full fancied flared tail during courtship, clutching a flask of wine and a chunk of bread, the symbol of blood and flesh amongst Christians, he approached the makeshift alter and gave the order to ring the bell loud and clear for, regardless of his limited knowledge of the Catholic ways, he'd give it his best shot.

Coincidently as it may seem, the instant Left Ear tuned in on the various earthly seismic vibrations, the bell boys, eager to follow orders to the letter, gave the rope a mighty heave, swinging the bell high, then back again, over and over, causing the bocce ball-sized cast iron clapper to repeatedly crash against the waist of the cast bronze bell, thus sending a powerful surge of vibrations surging through the metal, intensifying as they traveled through the sound bow, past the lip, thus emitting from the mouth of the bell in a thunderous bonging blast that echoed for miles. The surge of intense vibrations traveling towards the bell's crown where it was fastened to the yoke, likewise, in concentrate form, gathered and sped down the make-shift belfry (poles planted deep into the ground), now transformed into seismic vibrations which, at bullet speed whizzed the short distance to the far side of the rise, condensed in tight formations, and funneled into Left Ear's inner ear with devastating results. The homogenizing, paralyzing effect of this surge of power on the brain rendered him frozen in his squatting, head down position, and in trying to navigate in this stiffened form, bounced around more like a Mexican Jumping Bean than a Human Being, thus, at least for the present, putting an end to his brilliant tracking career.

Simultaneously, the unprecedented ear-splitting bonging sound waves, although somewhat tempered due to the deflection when striking the protective rise, but still powerful enough to shatter the quietness of the desert, surged into the group, thus stampeding the horses into galloping frenzy. Astounded, the Chief addressed his Medicine Man:

"What the hell was that??"

Before he could add to the statement, Left Ear came bouncing along, hopping over clumps of sagebrush like an overgrown cricket. In a state of shocked astonishment, the Chief asked:

"What the hell's the matter with him??"

Before he could add to the statement, he viewed his elite fighting force racing through the dust in hot pursuit of their stampeding steeds. Arms raised overhead, flailing the breeze wildly, his sun-baked skin drawn tight over protruding bones, with the horrifying expression of death warmed over, the Chief screamed:

"What the hell's going on here??"

The Medicine Man, being the only one with enough knowledge to comprehend a phenomenon of this nature, thunderous bonging echoing off the surrounding crags, believing this to be the doings of Spirits of sorts, or even some secret weapon of whatever nature, went into a crazy spiritual dance, rattling just about every gadget at his disposal while wailing and chanting frantically. The fact that he was obviously striking out on his own to save his own hide also brought about a disparaging comment from the Chief:

"You, too??" he asked. Then in a state of despair, shaking his head at the thought of having been defeated without so much as even seeing the enemy, let alone engaging him in battle, sat his fleshless, bony butt on a jagged rock and pondered his fate. Here he is, within grasp of achieving his goal, swoop down on the unsuspecting enemy, cart off the spoils of war, "vino," and his campaign falls apart for no logical reason.

As he sat there in near tears, he felt around for his salt scrotum; it was intact, thanks to the Spirits. It was apparent, they were now somewhat more sympathetic to his cause. Luckily, he was holding his Calumet when the horses stampeded. Another blessing. He carefully checked the array of feathers attached to it to be sure they were in proper sequence and undamaged. With two fingers he reached into the Calumet's companion pouch, the scrotum of a lamb, symbol of pureness, and retrieved the needed holy tobacco to complete the now inevitable peace offering. While tamping the tobacco into the pipe with his crooked finger (ideally suited for the purpose) in preparation of the peace offering, he pondered the question as to how to approach his adversaries since by the way things looked, all was lost and he'd have to go it alone.

But he wasn't alone. The Spirits of the Mountain, although

Dago Red! Westward - Ho!

at times they did indeed frown upon his unorthodox conduct, had now jumped in to lend a hand or, better put: guide him by first clearing the cobwebs out of his cluttered mind, then blasting it with a thought that rattled his bony frame from head to toe. He felt the power, the Spirits had scored. As if by spoken word, he received the message of salvation:

"Stay put! Wait!"

Bruno Buti

CHAPTER 16

The better part of an hour had gone by when finally, through the mirage-inducing heat waves floating above the desert floor, Chief Crooked Finger could make out the forms of horses with riders galloping towards him like Ghosts floating on air. "A Mirage," he thought, or maybe "Ghost Riders, the Spirits of the Mountain, coming down to kick his ass." But then, as the sound of pounding hooves reached his ears, he now knew that it was his own warriors, having caught up to their stampeding horses, they were coming back to his command. With renewed faith, he greeted his men with chants of praise as they reined their galloping mounts to an earth-churning halt. Sliding off their mounts, before the Chief had a chance to embrace any of them, his next-in-command, a Warrior-Commander, as unforgiving as he was mean, in a brisk gait strode over to the still dancing Medicine Man, and as he ranted and raved in a stooped position, the Commander, with as much determination as he could muster, booted him in the ass, thus sending him sprawling to the ground. Having gotten his attention, he now proceeded to berate him unmercifully:

"You and your stupid magic! Those damned horses where halfway back to camp before we could catch up to them!" he growled. "Now cut it out! Damn it!" he swore.

"No more of that . . . whatever the hell it was!"

Apparently amongst these plains Indians, mysterious phenomena of whatever nature were always the doings of the Medicine Man, either deliberately or inadvertently.

Therefore, the matter of a possible secret weapon was

ruled out. The Chief, being the Commander-In-Chief, praised and embraced his next in command, both for retrieving the horses and also for setting the record straight with the Medicine Man.

But now there was the matter of Left Ear, their official tracker, who at the moment, in one of his frantic attempts to overcome his paralysis, had flipped himself into a clump of brambles where he was struggling desperately to extricate himself. The Chief, without comment, with one arm raised and pointing, his other gnarled arm with the twisted, cockeyed, crooked finger of which his configuration as a whole didn't look much better than the sun-dried snags protruding from the patch of brambles that he was pointing at, let it be known that this was another urgent matter in need of attention.

The Commander, with full confidence instilled within him by the Chief, wasted little time in addressing the problem. Commandeering a half dozen warriors, they dragged Left Ear out of the brambles and without giving any thought as to what was causing the paralysis, ignoring the patient's screams and howls of pain, jerked, twisted, pushed and shoved until they had the patient straightened out to where he could at least stand on his two feet and, with the help of his comrades, was mounted onto his steed. Upon command, the others, including the Chief himself and the Medicine Man, as resentful as he was towards the Commander, mounted their steeds. A wave of hand set the attack in motion for now, at this point, it was a military matter, not civil. They followed their Commander willingly, up the slope of the rise to the ridge above.

Stretched out along the ridge of the rise, overlooking the encampment below, there stood this fierce-looking military force studying the layout and setting up the plan of attack. They'd give no quarter. They'd ask but once as to the whereabouts of the spring that produced the nectar of longevity, "wine." Unless divulged, torture, if not scalping, could be expected. They'd make no bones about their purpose for being there this day.

Riding hell bent for destruction, John came into view from down the lower end of the rise. Flushed with horror at the sight of the war party, he exclaimed:

"Oh my God! I'm too late!"

Paying no heed to the panting, sweaty condition of his horse, he spurred the frothing animal on. His intent was to get to the camp ahead of the war party and rescue Giuseppina lest she fall into the hands of the renegade Indians.

It was High Noon. The war party viewed the activity below. Long tables were set with much food, several barrels resting on freight wagons could be seen. These they knew contained drinking water as it applied to the pioneers, but now they knew differently, especially since there was a line up of people, young and old, men and women, goblets in hand, at one of the barrels resting on the tailgate of the wine wagon. Wine, not water, was pouring from its spigot. This was it; they'd scored.

At the instant the Commander raised his hand for the attack, the braves did likewise, while at the same time letting out a war whoop thus attracting the attention of the Italian inhabitants of the encampment below. In exulting enthusiasm, the Italians exclaimed:

"Look! Up on the hill! We have guests!" Excitedly they waved back and in their native tongue called out to the Indians to join them. Mistaking their actions as military, like their own, the warriors took up the challenge and charged down the slope. Once down the slope and onto the flat desert floor, the horses sailed over and through the sagebrush at full gallop. The Chief's feathered headgear, like the multicolored feathers of the rest of the war party, snapping to the winds of speed, coupled with the assorted designs of war paint adorning the bodies and faces of the warriors, in itself gave the impression of a carnival sports event of sorts. Thus the Italians waved their hats and cheered them on. But Reverend Gadwall knew differently:

"Oh my God! A war party! The wine!" he blurted as he beat it over to the wine wagon.

Elated that their offer to join them was accepted, the order was given to ring the bell, and to ring it loud, for this was indeed destined to be a joyous affair. And to better impress their God of Wine, Bacchus, adults, not children, took on the task of getting the most out of the cast bronze bell. With a mighty heave-ho, the bell rang out with a horrendous, repetitive blast of bonging, sending forth shock waves and vibrations the likes of which have never been produced since the walls of Jericho were reduced to rubble. The shock waves traveling at the speed of sound skimmed over the tops of the sagebrush on a head-on collision course with the on-coming frenzied, frothing, galloping horses. Merely yards short of the perimeter of the encampment, where polenta and baccala simmered in cast iron kettles and skillets suspended over open fires, and goblets of wine sat on food laden tables, the head-on collision between sound waves and horse flesh took place with devastating results. The horses bolted as if struck by lightening, and with hooves planted firmly to ground in a sudden abrupt dead stop, catapulted their riders through the air and into the sagebrush in a headlong, dust generating dive, ripping feathers off of them like plucking a turkey.

For an instant the Italians were horrified by the sight of the carnage that lay before them. To think that their guests were so eager to join them that, in their headlong dash to take their places at the table, they'd nearly destroyed themselves. To say the least, they were quite touched, but this was now an emergency. They must go to their aid, act quickly.

Fortunately, they knew what to do! Rushing forward with goblets of wine, they systematically but gently, while supporting their heads in cradled arms, first wet their guests' lips with wine, then as they regained their senses, encouraged them to drink heartily. Having previously experienced the goodness of this nectar of life, they did so with gusto, and eagerly!

Not having the same feelings towards their so-called guests as did the Italians, Reverend Gadwall in fear of losing the wine to the Indians, gun in hand, scrambled aboard the wine wagon, set the flint bearing cocks of the double barreled weapon, awkwardly took a defensive stance.

Assuming that a battle was taking place at the catastrophic, dust-obscured rescue arena, John's only thought was to find and get his Sweetheart Giuseppina out of there. Jerking the Winchester out of its scabbard, thumbing back the hammer, and while holding the gun up at the ready, he spotted her standing near the wine wagon, back to the wind as she'd been many times before, waiting for just such a moment. Coming in at full gallop, he reined his horse to a hoof-plunging stop directly in front of her and yelled:

"Grab my arm! Hang on!"

She obeyed, and in an instant was seated behind him. John sheathed his rifle then sank his spurs into the flanks of his frenzied horse, thus catapulting him into full gallop.

Whirling around to witness the event, Reverend Gadwell lost control of his ancient weapon. It toppled off the wagon with it's muzzles pointing upwards, cocks set in firing position, and in the course of it's decent, the gun's cocks struck the wagon tire thus causing a double barreled discharge.

In a horrendous, thunderous blast and dramatic spew of smoke and fire the likes of a belching dragon, one projectile ricocheted off the steel tire rim thus sending the lead ball ripping through the Reverend's baggy pants, creased his fat

Dago Red! Westward - Ho!

buttocks with an excruciating burning sting, and with enough of a bite to draw blood while the other projectile cleared the rim, thus continuing upwards whereas it punched a hole through the head of the wine barrel resting above the Reverend, thus bringing forth a gush of wine cascading down upon him. In a state of horrified shock, while grabbing at his seared, painful butt, the Reverend screamed:

"Oh! My God! I've been shot!"

As if that was not dramatic enough, he screamed again: "Oh! My God! The Wine! The Wine! Save the Wine!"

Concerned as the Reverend was about being wounded with his own gun and now the loss of the wine, left him little in the way of an option; he'd have to address both matters pronto. So, while maintaining a firm grip on his bleeding buttock with his left hand, he reached up and stuck the index finger of the other into the hole punched so neatly into the wine barrel by the projected lead ball. And so there he remained in this ridiculous, precarious position.

Within a matter of minutes the braves recovered from their ordeal. As a matter of fact, since they'd been plagued with mishaps and anxieties from the very start, they felt better now than before they took the dive. Even Left Ear, having been implanted headlong into a patch of sagebrush stiff as an arrow, and having been pulled back out in the same fashion as he went in, stretched out across the laps of a couple of robust bosomy Italian women, massaged with loving care as he sipped wine, like a miracle being performed in the presence of a Saint, limbered up from his paralysis. Thanks to the healing powers of wine and love, he was now fully recovered.

The Medicine Man, having been plucked clean of his array of colored feathers, divested of gadgetry and scrotums of mysterious powders, thus stripped of magical powers, walked arm and arm with the now more forgiving Commander, brought about by the sharing of the wine.

In the center of the gathering of these two extremely diverse ethnic groups, Chief Crooked Finger and the newly elected Italian Capo, Badolio, faced each other, holding goblets spilling over with wine, raising them high, clicking them together as they did so, and in unison, each in his own manner, with gestures and chanting, praised "Bacchus," the Roman God of Wine, and in a display of good fellowship, wished each other good health and longevity with a sincere, "Salute!"

The dust having cleared, John, looking back over his shoulder and seeing what appeared to be a victory for the Italians, reined his steed up short, swung him around with Giuseppina hanging on in a bear hug, squeezing the living daylights out of him. Her mother, Maria, having lost sight of her daughter due to the confusion, came running out from behind a wagon, frantically calling out her name:

"Giuseppina! Giuseppina! Where are you? Answer me! Where are you?"

Hearing the call, John reined his horse in Maria's direction, while at the same time shouting a response:

"Giuseppina is here with me! She's safe!"

Surprised to see John with her daughter clutching him, she exclaimed:

"Oh my God! She's on your horse!"

"Yes, and with your blessings, there's where she'll stay. I want your daughter's hand in marriage!"

Hands to her face, Maria again exclaimed:

"Oh my God! My Giuseppina!" Hesitating for a moment, she then added: "Well, it was her father's wish so . . . so be it!"

Eyes welled with tears of joy, Giuseppina sobbingly pleaded:

"John, I love you dearly. Please don't ever leave me again, for surely I will die if you do."

With the firmness of a Military Commander, he responded:

Dago Red! Westward - Ho!

"Don't you worry about that. It will never happen again!"

Trotting his horse back to the wine wagon, not really sure why the Reverend had struck this "Statue of Liberty" stance, posed a question:

"Are you a marryin' kind of Reverend?" he asked.

"Well . . . yes, I suppose so," came the answer.

"All right then, let's get with it, we're a marryín'!"

"Good grief, man . . . now . . . this instant?"

"Yes! Damn it, now!"

And that's the way it was, moving out west with a wagon load of "DAGO RED!"

End

The Wine Gnat's Plighted Troth

We wing our way following the wafting scent,
Of the wine maker's must as it ferments.

In his must we propagate faster than lightning and thunder,
What we lack in size we make up in numbers.

To the wine maker we Plight our Troth,
Were it not for his wisdom, perpetuity would be lost.

Wine vats and barrels is where we may be found,
During a barrel tasting, we're always around.

Good vintage, fine wine, you like it we trust,
This nectar derived from the winemaker's must.

Salute! To the bottom of the glass, quench your thirst,
Do as we gnats do, drink up until you burst!